THE FRONTIER BOYS :)

THE FRONTIER BOYS :)

JOHN GROOTERS

DESTINY IMAGE® PUBLISHERS, INC.
P.O. Box 310, Shippensburg, PA 17257-0310
"Promoting Inspired Lives."

This book and all other Destiny Image, Revival Press, Mercy-Place, Fresh Bread, Destiny Image Fiction, and Treasure House books are available at Christian bookstores and distributors worldwide.

For a U.S. bookstore nearest you, call 1-800-722-6774. For more information on foreign distributors, call 717-532-3040. Reach us on the Internet: www.destinyimage.com.

ISBN 13 TP: 978-0-7684-4114-7
ISBN 13 Ebook: 978-0-7684-8849-4

For Worldwide Distribution, Printed in the U.S.A.
1 2 3 4 5 6 7 8 / 16 15 14 13 12

For the Dew Brothers:

Jack Carlson, Pat Camilleri, Kurt Williams,
and Kirk Heckendorn

and how we once protected one another.

PROLOGUE

They say we only have two seasons up here in Northern Michigan: winter and road construction. I like the winter. It's basketball season. The town is pretty quiet, and the cold in no way prevents us from having a good time.

My best friends are Jackson, who talks a lot, Brent, who laughs a lot, and T.J., who is just the coolest guy I know. I know it sounds silly, but the four of us have a nickname. We're called The Frontier Boys.

—Jed Bracken

CHAPTER ONE

Brent Fencett was deep into nap sleep. On his back, on the couch, early in the afternoon, he was resting up before his high school varsity basketball game. The CBS broadcast of the Michigan State/Ohio State game was still on the TV, but Brent had long ago lost track of that. Suddenly, in the misty fog of his dreams, he heard the voice of Mike, his ornery 23-year-old brother, who was softly and gently calling his name. Brent was self-conscious enough to convince himself that he must be dreaming because Mike never spoke softly or gently to him. Insults, put downs, sarcastic comments – those he would recognize. But then his dream added another sensory dimension – suddenly he could smell his brother's smoky breath.

"Oh Brent. Oh Brenty-poo…" Mike Fencett drew his face to within an inch of his little brother. He was bent down by the couch where Brent was sleeping. His nose was practically touching Brent's ear. But Brent didn't stir, so Mike changed his tactics. He stood up, pointed his left elbow toward the center of Brent's stomach, dropped to the floor and thrust his elbow directly into the center of his sleeping brother's belly.

Oooph! As the air was knocked out of Brent's lungs, and he doubled up in startled pain.

"Oh good you're up." Mike said cheerily.

Brent, struggling to regain his wind, couldn't say anything.

"Where's my helmet?" Mike demanded.

Brent was disoriented from his nap and temporarily oxygen deprived, but he was coherent enough to know he had no clue where his brother's helmet was. He knew enough to never touch his brother's things.

"I, I have, I have no…" he couldn't get the words out. He had no air.

A toilet flushed down the hall. Brent glanced over and saw a dude he didn't recognize walking into the living room, a gap-toothed hillbilly-looking guy with crazy hair and beady eyes.

"Oh is this your little brother? He's so cute." The gap tooth said. "Mikey, were you ever this cute?"

"Not a chance," Mike answered.

"Mike, who is this guy?" Brent asked, the first words he managed to squeak out.

"Oh, hasn't your brother told you about his new friend Frank?" the gap tooth answered as he thrust his fist right up close to Brent's eyes.

Brent tried to focus on the fist three inches from his face. It looked like Mike's new friend Frank had given himself a bad tattoo across his knuckles, spelling out his name. Brent chuckled because apparently the gap tooth had not planned the space well, and had been forced to use his pinky knuckle for two letters: F – R – A – NK. Four fingers, five letters. Should have used the thumb.

"Nice, Mike," Brent said, trying to sit up.

"Brent, I've been meaning to ask you something," Mike said with mocking sincerity, "Where's my helmet?"

"What?" Brent sighed.

"Donde esta mi helmeto?"

"How should I know," Brent answered. "Where are you going?"

"Now he thinks he's your mom. You want to know what time he's gonna be home, too?" Frank said.

"I am going to…" Mike slugged Brent in the arm as hard as he could, "Painsville!"

He started singing like a crazy man.

"Then I'm gonna sing a song about punchin' you in the arm." He sang. "I just wrote that."

Brent slugged him back, right in the solar plexus. He hit him with his left since his right arm was temporarily in debilitating pain.

Mike was eight years older than Brent. He had tried college for about a semester, but dropped out and had since then been living back at home. Neither brother had seen their father, Mike Sr., in the six years since the divorce. Lois Fencett, Mom, was in the kitchen drying some dishes. She was usually oblivious to whatever was going on between her boys.

"Boys, be nice to each other," Lois offered helpfully.

"Mom, I need my helmet." Mike insisted.

"Oh your helmet? I picked it up honey," Mom answered. "It's in my car."

Mike abruptly got off the couch where he had been pinning Brent and headed through the kitchen toward the garage. Frank followed Mike like a puppy dog.

"Oh, Mrs. Fencett, that's a pretty sweater," Frank said with a childish tone of subtle derision.

"Why thank you," Mrs. Fencett answered – clueless to the sarcasm.

Brent tried to stand up. His arm and his stomach were hurting. He heard his brother's insanely loud motorcycle drive away.

"You have a game today honey?" Brent's mom asked from the kitchen.

Brent glanced at his own reflection in the living room mirror. He was wearing maroon and white varsity basketball warm-ups with a pair of white Adidas next to his feet. It occurred to him that his mom probably should have been able to surmise the answer to that question for herself. But she had never been adept at keeping track of his schedule, and so far this season she had not made it to any of his team's first nine basketball games.

So he just answered her question. "Yeah, it's a make-up game against Elk Rapids at 2:00. You comin'?"

"Yes, of course." Mom answered. "I'll try."

Brent knew she would not make it, and he told himself it shouldn't matter. She didn't understand basketball, and she would be embarrassed to go to the game by herself. Nevertheless, he wished she would come and watch him play. He knew she had gone to see Mike a couple of times when he played.

The double honk from the driveway indicated that his ride had arrived. Brent slipped on his boots, grabbed his Charlevoix

Rayder gym bag, walked to the kitchen and gave his mom a kiss on the cheek.

"Love you," he said.

"Good luck," she replied.

Rayder home games were played in the classic Charlevoix High gymnasium. Built in the early 60s and supported by huge arching beams, the gym looked more like an old time airplane hanger than one of the modern big box gyms most schools had. But its old school charm was why Brent loved it. The gym was big enough to hold two-thirds of the residents of the town, and most of them were there for every game.

At 2:02 PM the Rayder basketball team came bursting out the double doors from the hallway to the court, and the crowd rose to their feet with a great ovation. The pep band was blaring out a fight song, mostly on key, and Brent jogged through the gauntlet of cheerleaders waving pom pons. It was a glorious moment to be an athlete. All the running, all the practice, all the work throughout the summer paid off every time he ran out onto that court in front of the home crowd.

The Rayders were off to their best start in 20 years, and they were led by three fabulous sophomores. Brent and his best friends Jed and T.J. had not only all made the varsity team, all three were starting. And not only were they starting, they were winning! Nine games, nine victories. The team began doing a weave passing drill, where all twelve players were in constant motion. Basketballs flew back and forth, quickly touching one pair of hands then the next. The Rayders looked like the Harlem Globetrotters – continuous motion, constant energy.

This particular game was being played on a Saturday afternoon because the scheduled game had been cancelled due to a snowstorm. Snow-outs were not uncommon in Northern Michigan winters. The light in the gym was brighter than usual because daylight illuminated the white panes of semi-translucent glass that filled the arches at the top of each end of the gym. Typically these games were played well after sundown.

After six minutes of warm-ups, the buzzer blared. The teams gathered by their respective benches, and the PA announcer asked everyone to stand and the gentlemen to please remove their caps for the singing of the national anthem. Sports and patriotism are closely intertwined in American small towns like Charlevoix.

After the "home of the brave," the PA announcer fired up the crowd with a stirring introduction of the players.

"Ladies and Gentlemen, welcome to Charlevoix High for today's game between the Elk Rapids Elks and your Charlevoix Rayders! And now, starting for Charlevoix, at guard, a 6'2" sophomore, number 19, Jed Bracken!"

Jed shot off the bench and ran through the raised high fives of all his teammates. Jed was slender but muscular, broad shouldered, and handsome. He wore his hair about as short as he could cut it and looked like a thin young Marine. He had the steady and confident demeanor of a young man for whom things in life came easy. He jogged mid-court and shook the hand of the opposing coach.

"At forward, a 6'2 sophomore, number 44, Brent Fencett!" Brent followed Jed's path. His right arm was sporting a clearly defined black and blue bruise, compliments of his brother. Brent was thicker than Jed and he wore his hair longer. His hair naturally curled around and frizzed out, and Brent paid very little attention to where it went. After greeting the Elk Rapids coach he joined Jed on the court.

"You awake yet?" Jed asked.

"Not quite. I was having a pretty good nap," Brent answered.

Hayden and Lyndon joined Jed and Brent in the starting lineup, and then came Charlevoix's resident superstar. The crowd stood as the announcer milked his final introduction for all it was worth.

"And at point, a 6'1" sophomore, player of the week, number 23, T…J…. Lewis!"

The home crowd gave their loudest ovation. They loved T.J. There had never been a player in Charlevoix like T.J., at least for as long as anyone in the gym could remember. T.J. Lewis looked like a young Michael Jordan, and he played a bit like him too. It was no coincidence that he chose the number 23. T.J. was quick as a cat, but he could pull up on a dime and drain a jump shot from just about anywhere. Of course, he could also drive to the basket and dunk with such ease that the rim seemed only seven feet from the ground for him. Despite all his skill, T.J. was as humble as anyone you'd ever meet. He played the game with an easy smile, and was always the first in line to congratulate the other team. His personal motto was tattooed in small letters on the inside of his right arm: "grace and humility."

T.J. ran to meet his teammates in the middle of the court and was followed out by the rest of the members of the Rayder basketball team. They formed themselves into a tight and flowing circle, swaying back and forth with the energy and rhythm of a hip hop dance crew, bursting with the optimism and hope of a perfect season and a limitless future.

Then the game began, and as it turned out the other team came to play as well. In sports as in life, nothing good ever comes easy.

CHAPTER TWO

THE GAME WAS A DOGFIGHT. Midway through the fourth quarter, T.J. led all scorers with 24 points. Jed had added 16 more, and Brent had collected nine rebounds. But Elk Rapids was tough, and they had already drained thirteen three-pointers for the game. With only 00:14 to go the Rayders were down by one point, staring at the possibility of their first loss of the season. Coach Howell called his final timeout.

The raucous buzz of a packed gymnasium and the blasting brass of the pep band nearly drowned out Coach Howell's voice as the team huddled near the edge of the court. All five guys who had been playing sat on folding chairs; the rest of the team stood. Brent sat between T.J. and Jed. The Rayders were losing, but only by one measly point. Fourteen seconds was plenty of time to fix that – especially with T.J. Lewis on the team.

Jed wiped the sweat off his brow with his forearm and stared at Coach Howell, who was on his knees in the center of the circle of players. Coach Howell was confident, as always.

"Alright fellas, look at the clock," Coach said as he scribbled on his whiteboard, "We're down one; we got fourteen seconds to go. Jed, you inbound it. Brent, you're gonna set the screen. T.J.,

you're right there. The other two guys are just gonna go down and make sure we spread the floor out…"

Brent tried to pay attention to what the coach was saying, but he couldn't help glancing into the stands. He was still hoping he might spot his mom somewhere among the standing-room-only crowd.

"…We wanna get that shot off with just maybe a couple seconds to go," Howell continued. "On the shot, you guys gotta crash the boards. We're down one; we gotta come up with the rebound if it doesn't go in."

Brent looked at T.J. to see if he was nervous. T.J. was probably the only guy in the whole gym who wasn't nervous. He had a grin on his face. It didn't matter if everyone in the building knew that he was going to take the last shot to win or lose the game; T.J. never changed. He was just easy, confident, and cool. T.J. was going to take the last shot, and odds were pretty good he was going to make it.

Jackson Carlson sat in the stands just behind the bench. He wasn't actually on the team like his other three best friends, but Jackson considered his own contributions equal to, if not greater than, that of the players in determining the outcome of basketball games. In Jackson's mind the two most indispensable players for the Rayders were T.J. and himself, and T.J.'s position was tenuous.

Jackson, sometimes known as Jack the Mouth, proudly wore the mantle of most obnoxious cheerleader. His face was decorated with maroon and white war paint, he wore his lucky mustard-stained Rayders sweatshirt, and had a maroon pirate bandana tied around his head. At present he was standing with his back to the court leading cheers for the entire student section. He had the crowd screaming in unison, "Rayders, Rayders, woof, woof, woof!" over and over again. It made no sense. Jackson's cheers usually didn't. But on a cold Saturday in January, with the Rayders in first place and the game on the line, nobody cared. They just wanted to yell.

Brent, Jed, Jackson and T.J., collectively known as The Frontier Boys, were in their natural habitat.

:]

The boys were only ten years old when the legend of the Frontier Boys actually began. It was a Saturday afternoon in early autumn, and the four of them had spent the morning fishing off the long breakwater pier that jutted into Lake Michigan. The pier was a great place to catch fish. From their favorite spot the boys often pulled in trout, smallmouth and largemouth bass, a few perch, and an occasional walleye. The big prize, however, was salmon. During the fall spawning season, salmon would often congregate near the warm waters of the channel, and as holders of Michigan Department of Natural Resources' Young Angler's Fishing Licenses, the boys were legally able to fish for any species. That particular Saturday, Jed got the first hit.

At age ten Jed Bracken weighed all of sixty-five pounds; the big Coho Salmon he had hooked on his line was half as heavy as he was. Jed fought him for half an hour, letting out line, then reeling in when he could. When he got tired he handed the pole to T.J. After a while T.J. handed it off to Brent, and Brent eventually handed it off to Jackson. By the time they actually hauled the big salmon in with their fishing net, the boys thought they had landed Moby Dick.

Normally, they tossed the fish back after they caught them, but this haul was too good to be true. They didn't have a cooler to put the fish in. They had four poles, one net, and a plastic carton of salmon eggs, and now they had almost thirty pounds of salmon. Jackson, even at age ten, smelled profit.

"Let's sell him." Jackson said.

Jackson, who was husky even as a fourth-grader, bent down and cradled the big salmon in his arms like a newborn baby.

"Grab the poles boys," Jackson said. "We're takin' this baby to market!"

Each boy picked up his gear and began walking down the long concrete pier. They walked through the center of town carrying their still wiggly fish like a trophy. People stared.

By the time they made it to the front door of The Good Earth Coffee shop, Jackson was losing his grip on the fish. Nevertheless, they marched right inside and stood in a line before Bucky Potter.

Bucky was the owner of The Good Earth Coffee and Bagel Shop, and a friend and confidant to anyone who bellied up to his wooden bar and wanted to talk sports with him. The boys were regulars at the Good Earth, and had developed a particular taste for Orange Cream Sodas.

Bucky, staring at four boys, four fishing poles, a big fishing net, a tackle box, and a giant salmon, looked at them and asked, "What have you guys been doing?"

"Fishing!" They replied sincerely.

"Oh, I see—and what are you going to do with the fish?"

"Sell him," Jackson answered, "to you!"

"Oh, is that right? Sell him, huh. Well, how much do you want for him?"

The boys had not considered their price yet.

"Ten dollars?" suggested Jed.

"Jed!" Jackson interrupted, rolling his eyes. "One-hundred dollars."

Just then the big salmon slipped out of Jackson's hands, plopped down on the tile floor with a loud squish, and flopped around a bit.

It happened that the editor of the local newspaper, the Charlevoix Courier, was in the coffee shop that morning. He was amused by the entire scene, and he grabbed his camera and took a few pictures. He convinced the boys to pose outside the restaurant with their salmon. In a small town news can be hard to come by. The story was front page news.

The headline on the following Monday read:

Modern Frontier Boys?

> Like young pioneers scratching out a living on the wild frontier, local ten-year olds Jed Bracken, T.J. Lewis, Brent Fencett, and Jackson Carlson brought a fine 36-pound Salmon into the Good Earth Coffee Shop and General Store on Saturday, September 22, and offered the catch to store proprietor, Bucky Potter.
>
> Potter declined the offering, saying that The Good Earth didn't specialize in fresh fish, but offered that if the young fishermen could bring in a similar haul of Atlantic Lox, he would be happy to serve them with his bagels. He also asked the boys if they had any raccoon pelts they might be willing to exchange for cappuccino.
>
> Charlevoix can be proud of boys like these. The kind of courage and character demonstrated by our junior anglers harkens back to the proud days of Charlevoix's

settlement, when hardened men survived off the land and lakes. We can only hope that the spirit of the frontier is alive and well, even among a generation of fourth-grade boys from Charlevoix Elementary School."

Those four boys were no longer just boys and no longer just friends; now they had a nickname! The Frontier Boys.

:]

Fleeeep! The referee's whistle cut through the commotion.

"Any questions?" Coach Howell asked his players.

"Nope." Brent shook his head.

"All right, let's go!" Coach shouted.

As he stood, T.J. splashed water from his cup into Brent's unsuspecting face. Brent shook his head and laughed.

Man, T.J. feels no pressure, Brent thought.

The twelve players formed a huddle and put their hands together in the center. "One, two, three, TEAM!"

As the huddle broke and the players walked back toward the court, Coach Howell grabbed T.J. and pulled him aside.

"Hey, hey—you've been our guy all year; you go make it happen," Howell said. "Don't give me a heart attack; you just go finish the game for us."

T.J. smiled his easy smile.

As the teams walked back onto the court Jackson yelled from the stands, "Hey Brent—do *not* try be the hero. Just give the ball to T.J!"

Brent heard him. He couldn't help but laugh.

CHAPTER THREE

Downtown Charlevoix was defined by Main Street, the road that brought all travelers straight through the heart of town. Because Lake Charlevoix extended for seventeen miles to the east, and Lake Michigan was to the west, the only convenient way for travelers to drive north or south along Michigan's northwest coast was to go right through the center of downtown Charlevoix. Downtown looked like the back lot of a movie set designed to portray a charming, slightly historic, fishing village/resort town like Cape Cod, Massachusetts, or South Portland, Maine.

Some locals felt that winter was the only season when Charlevoix was its true self. In the summer the town swelled with tourists, visitors, and yacht clubbers – "fudgies" the locals called them. Though the summer visitors boosted the economy, some locals never liked sharing their town with the fudgies.

Mike Fencett never liked the fudgies. He couldn't stand the hassle the tourists brought every summer. Mike was born and raised in Charlevoix, had graduated from the public school system, and had come back after a brief but failed attempt at college. He was native, and by his way of thinking, the town owed him something for his loyalty.

Mike was one of the few locals not in the gym watching his brother play basketball. He never watched Brent play basketball. He couldn't stand to hear the crowd cheering for anyone else, least of all his little brother. He had been the star once. In his mind he still was.

It was wicked cold outside; Mike didn't care. The streets were dry, so he persuaded a couple of buddies to fire up their Harleys and race them through the streets. Mike was the starter, and he sat stationary on his own bike in the middle of the street with his hands high in the air. Two big Harleys revved up their four stroke engines and waited for Mike to give the signal. He pointed left to one rider, right to the other, and then dropped his hands. The two bikes catapulted forward right through the main street of town. Loud, fast, illegal – they could never get away with racing through downtown at any other time of the week. Mike was thrilled.

Mike liked to do things just because he thought he could get away with them. As the noise of the two big Harleys faded into the distance, Mike leaned back on the silver gas tank of his customized Buell 750 chopper, stared into the winter sky and smiled. He had bigger plans for this day than bike races though. He believed his luck was about to turn for the better.

CHAPTER FOUR

The scoreboard told the story. 00:14 left on the timer. Visitors 52, Home 51. Everybody was on their feet cheering. T.J. walked past Jed and slapped him on the butt as he walked back onto the court. The referee handed the ball to Jed and began to count down from five as he moved his hand in broad gestures up and down. T.J. broke hard to his left, into the backcourt. Jed flipped him the ball and raced toward the basket.

T.J. dribbled with his right hand across the timeline and cut to his right. He kept his body between the ball and the Elk Rapids player, and he kept his eyes up, looking at the other nine players on the floor. The lights on the game clock were flashing.

:12, :11, :10...

Jackson was screaming: Shoot the ball! Quit dribbling – you don't get points for dribbling! Shoot the ball!!!

But T.J. was in no hurry. He was just killing time. No reason to shoot too soon and leave any time on the clock for the other team.

The fans were counting in unison: "Nine, eight, seven...."

At six, T.J. made his move. He didn't look at the ball or at the hoop; he knew where both of those were. He only focused on the defender. He feinted to his right, and then with a quick-as-a-cat crossover dribble he jolted to his left, lost his defender, and rose into the air for a smooth-as-silk jump shot.

Once Brent saw T.J. break to his left, he turned and fought his way toward the basket to box his man out. He looked up; he saw the ball in the air. He fully expected to see the ball rip the net. It didn't. It bounced off the rim and away from him. A collective groan came from the sidelines. But almost instantly, cheers overrode the groan. The ref had his hand in the air. Foul. Brent hadn't even heard the whistle.

T.J. was going to the line with a chance to tie or win the game. The defender had plowed him over, and now, with two seconds left on the clock, the game would be decided by free throws.

Brent leaned in toward T.J. "Want me to take these for you?"

T.J. glanced at Brent and slowly shook his head.

Jed whispered in T.J.'s ear, "For such a time as this, right?"

"All right Esther," T.J. replied as he smiled.

The referee tossed T.J. the ball and gestured "two shots."

The crowd hushed as he took the ball. He dribbled once, flexed his knees, bounced slightly, and shot it.

Swish.

The crowd exploded. Tie game – only good things could happen with the next free throw. The home crowd again quieted in order to let T.J. concentrate.

Dribble. Bounce. Shoot. Swish. The people went berserk. Elk Rapids was out of timeouts, so they quickly threw a Hail Mary the length of the court. The ball landed in Brent's hands as the final buzzer echoed through the gymnasium.

Jackson nearly ruptured an artery in excitement. He was screaming, dancing, and rotating his arms like a wind up monkey. The players mobbed T.J., and students and parents poured out of the stands and onto the court. T.J. and Jed quickly lined up to shake hands and congratulate the other team.

"Good game, nice game, great game." T.J. was in front of the line, and Jed was right behind him, giving him a bear hug as he walked forward.

Final score: Charlevoix, 53, Elk Rapids: 52.

CHAPTER FIVE

AYLIGHT FADES EARLY IN NORTHERN Michigan winters, and by the time the game was over the afternoon sun was long gone. At the same time his little brother was showering and changing after the game, Mike was waiting in a deserted parking lot along the frozen shores of Lake Michigan for his recruits to show up. He had arrived plenty early. It was bitter cold, but Mike chose to keep his knit hat in his leather jacket pocket. He wanted to look tough—impervious to the elements. He had chosen this location intentionally. He thought the scene would impress his special guest. This particular parking lot sat next to the mighty Great Lake within the arc of the rotating light beam of Charlevoix's famous lighthouse. Every thirty seconds its light beams raked across the craggy white ice formations near the shoreline and swept over Mike's chosen location.

Mike was nervous and fidgety. He was nervous that Sean wouldn't show up, or that the guys he had invited wouldn't come. Mike had personally invited about a dozen guys to check out what he promised would be a "big-time opportunity," and he was eager to assume the role of gang leader.

Finally, one guy showed up. Big Mack was six foot five and 300 pounds. His football career was cut short when he was suspended from his college team for using steroids.

"Hey," Mike said while playfully punching Big Mack in the arm, "You're gonna be real glad you came out tonight."

"I better be," said the giant.

Frank Snelling showed up on his motorcycle. He was freezing, and clearly just as nervous as Mike was. Frank couldn't stand still, even for a second. He was prancing around the frozen parking lot like a nervous Chihuahua, jabbering to nobody in particular, talking as if words themselves would keep him warm. Mike knew he could get Frank to do anything, and Frank Snelling had been the first one Mike recruited.

The parking lot was filling up with vehicles. The exhaust fumes from the trucks and bikes made the whole scene look like a gathering of dragons. The pick-up trucks, motorcycles, and cars kept their engines running and their lights on. Eventually eleven guys were standing out in the criss-crossing light, smoking cigarettes and drinking beers. Sean was nowhere to be found. The guys were starting to lose their patience.

Mike relented and pulled his black stocking cap over his head. He still tried to act like he wasn't cold. It was almost 7 o'clock, and he'd been expecting Sean at 5:30. Mike had actually only met Sean once in person, but he had bragged about him to his friends like they were tight.

Finally a shiny chocolate brown Audi Q-7 pulled around the corner and eased into the parking lot. The LCD headlight pattern looked like cats eyes as the SUV quietly crept down the drive. The Audi came to a stop and sat still for a moment. Nobody moved. Then, almost silently, the driver's door opened, and a tall bearded driver in black leather got out and walked around to open the back door on the passenger side. Slowly, a short guy in a brown leather coat extracted himself from the car. He wore an Irish bowler hat and had a tight black beard and even blacker eyes. The driver stood holding the door. The bowler hat stood and surveyed the scene. He was apparently in no hurry.

Mike was relieved, and energized. He hopped up on the flatbed of his pickup truck and whistled through his frozen lips. The whistle wasn't much, but it did the job.

"Hey guys, you know that contact I was telling you about? Well the man has arrived. Elvis is in the building, and he's as high as it gets in the drug world—no pun intended." Mike paused. He had rehearsed this. "I welcome you to the land of opportunity. This will be a night you won't soon forget."

"Get down from there, Michael," the man in the hat said. He sounded like he was from Eastern Ireland. His accent was thick. "Hello boys."

Mike stood still on the back of the truck. He hadn't finished his speech. Sean O'Sullivan glanced at him again.

"Mike, I'm serious. Get down."

Mike sheepishly hopped off the truck, and a couple of guys chuckled. Sean got right to the point.

"I'm here for one reason. Money. We are moving in, and we will control the action. Now Michael here tells me he can get me a few good men. Consider this an audition. If I like ya, I'll hire ya—and you will make a lot of money. It's very simple."

"We're going to take over distribution," Mike piped in. "It should be us controlling things around here anyway."

Sean stared at the guys around him. He was naturally skeptical, and inherently cautious. Sean had contacted Mike Fencett to see

if a drug distribution ring could be set up using local guys. Sean didn't trust a single one of them, and expected the audition to go poorly. But, he had come a long way. Maybe he'd get lucky. For a long time no one moved, aside from a few additional slurps on the beer cans and a couple long drags on cigarettes.

Finally Frank spoke up. "What do you mean audition, what kind of audition?"

Sean walked slowly toward the Frank. "Stick around and you'll find out. Or walk away right now."

"Man, we're here ain't we?" Frank answered with a snicker.

Sean stared at him with black eyes that saw no humor in the situation. He walked right up and spoke firmly but quietly right to his face. "Yes, indeed you are. But are you any good? Are ya? Well that's what I'm aimin' to find out."

Nobody moved. Nobody walked away. Mike's makeshift gang was curious.

Frank let out a nervous laugh. "So what, exactly, we gotta do?"

CHAPTER SIX

THE HALLWAYS OUTSIDE THE GYMNASIUM were buzzing with students and parents. People lingered longer after a victory, and after a tenth straight victory nobody was in a hurry to leave. Jackson was waiting in the hall just outside the locker room door.

Brent came bursting out of the locker room with his hair wet and his maroon and white gym bag slung over his shoulder.

"Ladies and gentlemen—Brent Fencett!" Jackson said looking into an imaginary television camera. Jackson was speaking into a rolled up score sheet as if it were a microphone, acting like he was actually doing a live post game television interview. The girls in the hall were amused. "Three steals, nine rebounds, and no stupid shots. For him, the perfect game. What do you have to say about this stunning victory?"

"Thank you, thank you," Brent said. "Are we live?" Brent glanced around the hallway. There were plenty of other parents and students milling about, but no sign anywhere of his mom.

"No—we're not live—actually," Jackson put his hand up to his ear, as if someone were speaking to him through an earpiece. "Upstairs wants a bigger name." Jackson glanced toward the

locker room door as Jed and T.J. emerged. Jackson brushed Brent to the side and approached T.J.

"T.J. Lewis, is it true? America wants to know. After tonight, are you ready to declare yourself the first high school student to ditch the tenth grade and jump straight to the NBA?"

T.J. grinned his big toothy grin as he leaned in to speak into Jackson's paper microphone. "Um, no, no," he answered, "I value my education more than millions of dollars, shoe endorsement deals, or international fame. I'm definitely staying right here, at Charlevoix High School where I plan to graduate from the tenth grade, something no one will ever be able to take from me. Thank you."

Brent leaned in from behind so the "cameras" could see him and said, "I'd take the money."

T.J.'s father, Reverend Lewis, came around the corner. Brent noticed his cologne. T.J. was wearing the same thing. Stereo cologne.

"Good game boys," Reverend Lewis said in his deep booming voice. "Brent, great game. On my scorecard, your man only scored one point on you today. Great job!"

T.J.'s dad was an impressively sized man. Reverend Lewis had earned the nickname Earthquake during his days as a boxer. He was a former heavyweight who had competed for the U.S.A. in the 1984 Olympics in Los Angeles. He still looked like he could step into the ring. Six foot four and tough as nails, he told stories of how Mike Tyson and Michael Spinks refused to even spar with him because he hit so hard. Now a pastor, his manner was mild and sincere, but no sane person would dare to mess with him.

"Thanks," Brent said. "But we couldn't have done it without our faithful mascot—Jackson."

"Well, lets give credit where credit is due," Reverend Lewis laughed. "Nice game Jackson."

"Thank you, Reverend. I was actually surprised Elk Rapids dared to take the court after the brutal heckling I gave them in warm-ups. They just about turned around and went straight back to their bus."

Reverend Lewis wrapped his son in a bear hug. "Good game, big shot," he said quietly.

"Thanks, Dad," replied T.J., hugging him right back.

Jed's mom and dad, Kevin and Judy Bracken, rounded the corner and met the boys.

"Nice game, guys," Jed's mom said with an ear-to-ear grin.

Jed's mom Judy was a beautiful Australian-born brunette. She was gracious and sincere and had a smile that could light up a room. Jed's dad, Kevin Bracken, was a tall southerner with a long ponytail and a gregarious personality who loved life, loved his family, and was always fun to be around.

"You guys winnin' like that is makin' it harder and harder to get a decent seat anymore," Jed's dad deadpanned as he gave his son a big hug.

"Yeah, sorry about that, Dad."

"Oh, the gymnasium's just too small. I keep telling them they're gonna have to put in those luxury boxes if they even want to compete in this conference!"

Jed's mom smiled, "Luxury boxes?"

"Got to keep up with the revenue, right?" Jackson piped in. "And hey, speaking of revenue, how come you never throw us the pocket change anymore?"

Pocket change. Jed's dad had a playful habit of asking them if they had any pocket change. Of course they always said, "No." Mr. Bracken would fill their pockets with change. To the boys, he was King Midas.

"You need some pocket change again, son?"

"You know, now that you mention it…," said Jackson, scouring his own pockets. "I could've sworn I did have some. Now where did that go?"

Mr. Bracken laughed and pulled out a few coins.

"Of course, this has nothing to do with basketball," he said as he handed the spare change to the guys, "I don't want anybody losing their amateur status."

Brent looked down at the quarter in his hand. "I'm not worried."

Kevin Bracken smiled. Then he pulled out a few real dollar bills and handed them out. "Ah, knock yourselves out."

"Now that's what I'm talking about," Jackson said.

"Jed, I like your dad," Brent added.

"You guys need a ride?" Jed's mom asked.

"No, that's okay; we're all right. We'll walk," T.J. said.

"It's like ten degrees outside," Jed's mom warned.

"It'll be okay, Mom. It's tradition," Jed answered. "Can you take this?"

Jed slung his gym bag over his mom's shoulder, and Brent did the same. Mrs. Bracken chuckled and took on both bags. T.J. gave his to his dad.

And with that the boys were free. Victory, a couple bucks in your pocket, your best friends, and a Saturday night before you was about as good a combination as any teenager could ask for. They would walk downtown, as always, regardless of the temperature. It was their personal victory parade.

CHAPTER SEVEN

SEAN O'SULLIVAN OPENED THE REAR hatch of the Q-7 and grabbed a stack of note cards. On each of them he had written a list of items that he needed to set up a crystal methamphetamine cooking lab. Each of the items, by themselves, seemed benign. Propane gas, plastic funnels, tables, glass mixing jars, a freezer, matchbooks, antifreeze, and lots of allergy and cold medicines. Put together they could be transformed into a dangerous and combustible lab that would make the highly addictive and highly profitable street drug known as ice, meth, or crank.

"You boys ready to go on a little treasure hunt?" Sean asked Mike.

"We are, Sean. My guys are ready for this," Mike answered. "You'll see."

"Good. We'll start small," Sean answered. "Get the stuff. Don't get caught. When you prove you can handle small things, then we move on to bigger ones."

Sean pointed to a truck tucked away in the darkness at the edge of the parking lot. "Load it up. Truck pulls out at first light. Those of you who deliver will earn your first payday."

For a moment, nobody moved.

"What are ya nancies waitin' for – Go!"

:)

It was a cold night with a light snowfall in the air. T.J., Brent, Jed, and Jackson walked down the hill on the south end of town. T.J. and Jed were wearing their deep maroon letter jackets with cream-colored leather sleeves. The big white varsity "C" was still a badge of honor in Charlevoix. Brent didn't have a letter jacket – not because he hadn't earned the letter, but because he hadn't had the money to buy one.

Traffic in the early evening was steady, and Jed was calling out car models based on the shape of the headlights he saw approaching in the distance. Jed was good with cars. The next set of headlights appeared. Jed pointed.

"Nissan Armada," he declared.

"No way. You can't tell a car by its headlights," Jackson answered.

Moments later a silver Nissan Armada drove past.

"Nissan Armada!" said Brent, as he punched Jed in the shoulder.

"Lucky guess," Jackson said.

Jed looked ahead at the next set of lights coming in the distance. He pointed again. "I'd say - Audi A-4."

"I'm going with an 18-wheel Mack truck pulling a semi," Jackson offered.

Moments later a black sedan whizzed by.

"Oh, it's an A-6," called Brent. "You lose!"

Jed laughed out loud. He was proud of that call. The A-4 and the A-6 were nearly identical.

From the behind them to the south, the boys heard a distant rumble. Something loud was coming, and it was coming fast. Jackson fell down onto the ground and put his ear to the pavement, like a Cherokee Indian scout.

"Do you hear that?" Jackson asked as if only he could detect the oncoming thunder.

The noise was so loud windows were practically rattling.

"Sounds like we've got the Blessing of the Bikes comin' to town."

The deep and throaty potato-potato-potato sounds of three massive Harley's followed by one low-hung Buell 750 chopper came roaring down the hill and raced through the main street of downtown. None of them, apparently, could afford mufflers.

"Whoa!" yelled T.J. as the bikes disappeared to the north. "Who rides bikes in January?"

"Idiots," said Brent shaking his head. "Freezing idiots."

CHAPTER EIGHT

THE GOOD EARTH COFFEE SHOP was the boys' favorite hangout spot. Any time they had pocket change, it was soon traded for mochas, smoothies, hot chocolates, or orange cream sodas at The Good Earth.

The Good Earth had a comfortable and casual interior: knotty pine walls, a well-worn tile floor, an antique woodstove, and a unique collection of fishing lures, knick-knacks, and used CDs for sale all around the store. The best part of The Good Earth was the long wooden counter serviced by four high top bar stools. That was the only place to sit, as far as the boys were concerned. It made them feel like they were bellying up to the bar in an old western saloon. Plus, the bar stools had the best view of the TV.

The bell on the door announced all new arrivals. Bucky looked up from his perch behind the bar where he'd been watching the Red Wings on the TV.

"Well, if it ain't the Frontier Boys," Bucky called out as soon as the door opened. "I could smell ya before I saw ya."

"Awe, c'mon now, Bucky. We showered." Brent answered.

Jackson sniffed his own armpits.

"Aargh - I didn't." Jackson quickly retorted. "And I worked up quite a lather at that game."

As the boys sat down Bucky was already popping the tops off four bottles of Henry Weinhards Orange Cream Soda. "I had the radio on; I heard the whole thing today. This one's on me," Bucky offered.

"You don't have to do that, Bucky." T.J. said. "Jed's dad gave us the pocket change."

Bucky laughed. "Just put it in the tip duck. Nice face paint, Jackson. I think you look better in disguise."

"Oh yeah? I could paint you. Maybe smooth over some of those wrinkles."

Bucky laughed. "You boys made me a bit nervous tonight there at the end."

"Well, good thing I brought my 'A' game then, huh?" Jackson bragged.

"Apparently, Jackson almost scared 'em off in warm-ups!" Jed said.

"Tell me about the end. Fourteen seconds to go, down by one point. Were you guys nervous?" Bucky asked.

"I was scared out of my boots, and I'm pretty sure I wet myself," Jackson said.

Bucky laughed. "How about you, T.J.? Do you get nervous stepping up to the line, the game in your hands to win or lose?"

"I was a little nervous," T.J. admitted. "I would have rather just made the jump shot to tell you the truth."

"Yeah, except the guy from Elk Rapids tried to dismember you when you went to shoot," Jackson said.

"I offered to take the free throws for him," Brent offered.

"Which was a great idea, since you make about one out of every seven free throws you attempt," Jackson said.

"You know, in my day, the proper way to convert a free throw was with the underhand toss."

Bucky stepped back from the bar and pantomimed an underhand free throw. Hands below the waist, knees bent, a gentle toss forward. This made Jackson laugh.

"The underhand toss? Yeah, in your day they wore the short shorts too, didn't they?" Jackson joked.

"Hey," Bucky replied, "there was nothing wrong with our shorts. At least we knew they were shorts! And besides, Rick Barry, who still has the best free throw percentage in NBA history, shot 'em that way."

There was a time when the boys might have just accepted a statistic like that as actual fact. Jed, however, was less trusting, and he did a quick internet search on his phone for NBA free throw percentage.

"Nope, not Rick Barry," Jed said. "Mark Price—90.4%."

"Hmm," Bucky answered. "Mark Price – you sure?"

"Yup," said Jackson, "And you know what he was wearin'?"

The four boys answered in unison, "Short shorts." Everybody laughed.

"I was actually hoping he'd miss the second free throw so I could slam dunk the rebound," Brent said. "Then maybe Jackson would have interviewed me after the game."

"It's a good thing you made 'em, T.J.," Jackson said. "The only thing Brent could dunk is a donut."

"I'm Tim Duncan to you pal," Brent retorted.

"These guys all played great." T.J. said. "I'm sure Brent would have dunked the rebound if I had missed. We were lucky to win."

"Don't believe in luck," said Jed.

"Good point; me neither. We were 'fortunate' to win," T.J. said.

"We were 'fortunate' I didn't run out and body-slam that guy who tackled you on that last-second shot. I was ready to cold cock that guy!" Jackson said. "That wasn't a foul; that was aggravated assault."

Jed chuckled. "Jackson, you're gonna harm the fine reputation of our school sooner or later."

"I *am* the reputation of the school." Jackson answered.

"If you were the reputation of our school," Brent added, "We would have no girls in the entire school. We'd be an all boys academy."

"Are you kidding me?" Jackson answered. "Most of the girls in our school transferred in just to watch me learn."

On cue the bells on the door jingled and a group of girls from the school came inside.

"See what I mean?" Jackson looked over his shoulder at them, "Isn't that right, ladies? The only reason you live in Charlevoix is because I'm here."

"Of course, Jackson," one of the girls replied. "You're the meaning in my life."

Under his breath, Jackson said to Jed, "I think she's serious about that."

"So what is that," Bucky asked, "nine straight wins?"

"Ten straight, as in 10 and 0!" corrected Jackson. "Conference championship in sight. I'm starting to get calls—*Sports Illustrated* wants these guys for a cover—course, I refuse. Don't want to jinx the season… Wait, hold on—I think I'm getting a call now."

Jackson picked up a plastic yellow mustard bottle, put it to his ear, and began speaking into it as if it were a cell phone. He put his hand up to cover the mouthpiece and loudly whispered to Bucky, *"It's ESPN the Magazine."*

"Yes, yes, sure. We would consider a photo session for you," Jackson said, speaking directly into the mustard, "If the price is right, of course. Have your people call my people, 'kay? Bye."

If verbosity had been a high school sport, Jackson would have been all state.

CHAPTER NINE

SUDDENLY, THE INTERIOR OF THE restaurant rumbled as the sound of four extremely loud motorcycles cruised through the downtown streets. The sound of motorcycles was unnatural in the middle of winter. T.J. slid off his stool and walked toward the windows.

"Is that your brother on one of those bikes?" T.J. asked Brent.

"Could be." Brent answered vaguely.

Just then T.J.'s father and sister arrived. "My oh my—it sure feels better in here," T.J.'s dad announced as he stepped inside the Good Earth."

"Hey," T.J. said, "You're not following me are you now?"

Reverend Lewis laughed a little. "Of course not. I'm just here to bring your sister to the best mochas in town."

From behind the counter Bucky shouted proudly, "In any town!"

T.J. went over to greet his dad and give his sister a hug. Jed followed and peered around T.J.'s back, "You proud of your little brother tonight?" he asked Jordyn.

"Every night, and not just because he can play basketball." Jordyn replied with a bright smile.

T.J. and Jordyn were about as tight as a brother and sister could be. Their mother had died when Jordyn was nine and T.J. was seven. Ever since then, Jordyn had tried to fill the roles of both sister and mother for her little brother.

Rev. Lewis did the best he could as a single father. He had legendary strength, and all the boys loved it when he played basketball or football with them. T.J. was proud of him. For T.J., the word *father* had many positive connotations. Unfortunately, he had much less experience with the word *mother.*

Jed and T.J. moved to the C.D. station and put on the headphones while Reverend Lewis and Jordyn took their places on the barstools. Reverend Lewis sat next to Jackson.

"You preachin' tomorrow, Reverend?" Jackson asked.

"My goodness, is tomorrow Sunday again already?" Reverend Lewis replied.

Jackson shook his head. "You know, you really should learn the value of preparation. We talk about it all the time in Boy Scouts."

"You, a Boy Scout?" Rev. Lewis chuckled. "Jackson, you're welcome at the church any time, but the Boy Scouts? Come on, they have standards!"

"Hey, I could be an Eagle Scout," Jackson said with a pout, "If I wanted."

"Yeah, and I could be Michael Phelps, too," Reverend Lewis said.

"Olympic champion or boring preacher—you probably should have gone with swimming," Jackson laughed at his own wit.

Reverend Lewis took his enormous hands and grabbed Jackson in a headlock. "You talkin' smack to me?"

"Hey, abuse, abuse!" Jackson cried out.

Reverend Lewis let him go. "Man, you wouldn't know what abuse is."

"I've sat through some of your sermons," Jackson retorted, laughing.

This actually made Reverend Lewis laugh, too. He looked at Bucky. "What are you gonna do with this guy? Such an insolent generation."

Bucky just smiled and shrugged his shoulders.

At that moment Frank Snelling, the gap-toothed hillbilly, walked into The Good Earth. Frank had frizzy hair and beady eyes. He wore a green army surplus jacket and military boots. He was nervous and jumpy, and he smelled like he worked in a cigarette factory. He loitered near the door, unsure if he was going to stay or go.

Bucky, from behind the counter, asked, "Can I help you?"

"Nope." Frank replied, but he didn't leave the store. He didn't sit down either. He just lingered.

Bucky turned his attention back to the hockey game on the television as Frank wandered aimlessly about the store. Eventually Frank approached the rack of used CDs. He glanced around and tried to act casual. Then, when he was sure nobody was paying any attention to him, he discreetly slipped a couple CDs into his coat pocket and headed straight for the door.

But T.J. was paying attention. He saw the whole thing go down. As soon as Frank stepped out the door T.J., without a word to anyone, followed right after him. Frank was ten paces down

the sidewalk when T.J. put his left hand on Frank's left shoulder and firmly spun him around. Even though T.J. was eight years younger than Frank, he stood eye to eye with him.

In a direct but non-threatening tone T.J. looked Frank square in the eye.

"You're gonna pay for those, or you're gonna put them back."

Frank was stunned for a moment and at a rare loss for words.

The temperature was now less than ten degrees. Standing on the sidewalk in that kind of cold meant that every word carried visible breath, breath that was backlit by the light from the windows of the Good Earth. Standing toe to toe Frank wondered if Earthquake Lewis' son could fight like his old man. He quickly decided he didn't want to find out. Frank adopted a cocky expression and leaned in as if to touch noses with T.J.

"You talkin' to me?" He said with attitude.

"You heard me," T.J. said calmly.

Frank fidgeted. He wasn't quite sure what to do. For one thing, it was freezing outside, and he was cold. For another thing, Frank was a natural born liar, and his first inclination was to simply deny he had taken anything to begin with. But he knew the kid must have seen him do it.

"Who do you think you are kid? You can't tell me what to do," Frank said, trying to sound tough.

But T.J. held his ground and kept his eyes locked on Frank's.

"What are you gonna do? You gonna call the police? You gonna call your daddy? You gonna nark on me, man?" Frank said.

"Just pay for those, or put them back. We'll have no problems here." T.J. said.

Frank rocked back and forth. He tried to match T.J.'s stare, but he just couldn't. He glanced at the ground. Frank loved to talk tough, but he knew in his heart he wasn't really tough. For a moment he pondered the possibility that T.J. might actually beat the tar out of him. That would be unbearably embarrassing, especially now that he was in a big-time gang. Finally he pulled the CD's out of his coat pocket and dropped them to the pavement.

"Fine. Fine." He said as he dropped the CD's and turned to walk way. Once he was safely out of T.J.'s reach he added the insult, "You're gonna regret this, boy."

T.J. watched Frank walk away before he bent down and picked up the CDs. He walked back into The Good Earth, put them back on the rack where they had been, and sat down again at the bar. He didn't say a word about what had just gone down. Brent didn't need to ask. He had seen the whole thing.

CHAPTER TEN

AT 11:00 PM SATURDAY MIKE was in his garage working on his motorcycle. He left the garage door open, and the jet powered space heater blasting. The Fencetts had a two-car garage, and Mike took both spaces—one for his truck, the other for his motorcycle. His mom parked her minivan outside on the driveway.

Mike was working on his silver Buell 750 custom chopper. His bike was totally impractical. It had no shocks, no fenders, and a super fat rear tire; it was horribly uncomfortable and barely street legal. None of that mattered to Mike, however, because it was about the coolest-looking bike he had ever seen. With its short exhaust and non-existent muffler, the Buell was also as loud as a drag race car. Mike liked that too. He liked the attention.

Mike's first night as would-be gang leader had been a huge success. Sean had seemed pleased with the amount of stuff they had collected. They had practically filled an entire truck worth of meth lab supplies. If everything came together on schedule, they would be fully operational within twenty-four hours. This thing could work. Sean would surely keep Mike in leadership over his guys, and Mike's cut of the profits would be substantial.

It wouldn't be long till he could move out of his mother's house and establish himself on his own.

"Thanks for the ride, Mr. Bracken. See you later." Brent hopped out of the Bracken's car and shuffled down the dark driveway toward the light pouring from the open door of the garage. Mike looked up as Brent approached.

"Why do you leave the door open? You're wasting heat." Brent said to Mike.

"Why do you act like such a female...girl?" Mike retorted.

"Nice Mike." Brent paused, content to just leave well enough alone and get in the house. But he was curious. He had to ask. "Mike, what's going on?"

"Nothing's going on."

"I saw you tonight; something's goin' on."

Mike mocked Brent's voice, "Oh, my name's Brent. There's something goin' on around here." Mike had the uncanny ability to sound like he'd just swallowed a mouthful of helium.

Brent picked up a basketball off the floor and hit the garage door opener, sending the door back down.

"Hey! I want that open," Mike protested.

"Huh?" Brent pretended not to hear.

He was about to walk in the house, when he turned back around and asked, "Why are you hanging out with Frank?"

"What are you, my girlfriend?" Mike said.

"No, I just—I saw Frank tonight. He was liftin' CD's at Bucky's."

"Wait, CDs?" Mike laughed, "That's weak."

"He's a punk, Mike. You should stay away from that guy."

"Thank you Dr. Brent. I'll call you next time I need advice on the stupid line."

Brent shook his head and stepped toward the door, but Mike stopped him.

"Hey, could you grab me the 5/8 socket?" Mike called out.

Brent dug through the toolbox in the corner of the garage and found the socket. "This one?"

Mike looked closely at it. "Perfect."

Brent paused for a moment behind Mike to watch him. As much as Brent couldn't stand his brother, he had always admired his mechanical skills.

"I've got a little something going on right now. Could be something big. Can't tell you about it though." Mike said.

"Can't tell me about what?" Brent asked.

Mike paused. "Now that's a bright question. 'Can't tell me about what?' If I told you what I can't tell you about, then I guess I'd have told you, genius."

Brent sighed. Trying to have a normal conversation with Mike was rarely worth the effort.

"Whatever." He said, turning to go into the house. "Just be careful."

"I've been careful my whole life, and look where that got me. I think it's time I stopped being so careful."

Brent paused by the door. "Wait. That's why you're hanging around with Frank? Didn't he get arrested or something once? You have a little something going on with Frank? That's brilliant."

"Oh, you're brilliant, my little Einstein. Frank is fine. He's part of the plan."

Now Brent was intrigued. "What plan?"

"When did you get so pushy?"

Brent held the basketball and paused by the door. "I'm not pushy," Brent said, "I'm just curious."

"Well, if you're really that curious, guess I could tell you a little." Mike thought for a moment. "Maybe you could even be useful."

"Useful for what?" The thought of being useful to Mike was strangely appealing. His big brother hadn't had any use for him in years.

Mike stood up. He was greasy from working on his bike, and he kept a wrench in his hand. "Brent, there's more to life than just basketball. Look at me; I'm way better than you'll ever be, and the game's still over for me."

"C'mon. You know what? I'm pretty good at basketball," Brent said.

"It doesn't matter; it will never pay. I'm talking about something that will pay."

Mike sat back down on the short stool by his bike.

Brent paused, and then asked, "How much pay?"

"A lot of pay."

"Is it legal?" Brent asked.

Mike ignored the question. "Tell you what. Tomorrow I'm going to be meeting with some guys. You want to find out what's up? I'll bring you along, let you decide for yourself."

Brent hesitated, "But I've got church tomorrow."

Mike threw up his hands, "Oh, well, then… never mind," he said mockingly.

Brent paused. He usually spent Sunday afternoons at Jed's house, and Jed's mom always made a fantastic meal.

"How about after church?" he asked.

Mike nodded. "Fine."

CHAPTER ELEVEN

O N SUNDAY MORNING REVEREND LEWIS orchestrated two ser-vices at the Community Church of Charlevoix. He was the first black pastor in Charlevoix, and the church he served was 99 percent white. Didn't matter. Reverend Lewis believed he was working right where God had called him.

Jed and T.J. were regulars at the 11 o'clock service. Sometimes they could convince Jackson and Brent to join them. None of the boys, however, had ever attended the 9:30 service. It was physically impossible for any of the four of them to wake up before 10 a.m. on Sundays.

Reverend Lewis preached with passion. "Bad company corrupts good character" was his theme for the morning. CCC was the kind of church that worked hard to be as easy and inviting as possible. It wasn't the oldest, it wasn't the newest. The sanctuary itself may have been contemporary once, but that would have been in the 1960s. Despite its traditional architecture, the church had a great band and a full house. Jed liked to belt the songs out at the top of his voice; he had no inhibitions. Brent was a little more self-conscious.

When the last song of the morning ended, Reverend Lewis raised his hands for the benediction - the final blessing - and a few final thoughts.

"Be people of grace, patient with one another, kind and loving. And may the Lord bless you, may his face shine upon you, and give you peace. Amen. God bless you, have a beautiful week."

That was the cue for people to leave, and for the music to start. But an instant before the first note, Butch Kooyer, the church youth group leader, frantically waved his hands and caught Reverend Lewis' attention; there was one forgotten announcement.

"Skating rink—tonight, at the rink." Butch held up a stack of flyers he had printed.

"Oh yes, one more thing," Rev. Lewis said, "I almost forgot - tonight at seven the youth group is going to be at the skating rink. It's going to be a great time. Be there at the skating rink. God bless you."

The band kicked in and the congregation filed out of the sanctuary.

Butch hustled to the back so he could pass out his flyers. Butch was a part time youth leader. His specialty was organizing events and activities for the teens. He was only a few years removed from the teens himself. "Games of pain, games of skill. Bring your blades, bring your wheels. 7 o'clock tonight. Skating rink." Jed and Brent walked past Butch and took copies of his flyer.

"Prizes?" Jed asked as he looked over the information.

"Yes, there will be prizes," Butch said to Jed. "But now you are disqualified. You can be a judge with me."

"Perfect." Jed smiled.

Butch knew that Jed was an amazing skater. If there was any kind of skating competition and Jed was in it, not many others would bother trying.

Jed, Brent and Jackson walked out the doors of the church still looking at Butch's flyer. On this Sunday the temperature was low, but with no wind it was tolerable to be outside.

"This looks interesting," Brent said.

"I hope Butch remembers to turn the heat on," Jed said.

Jed's dad, Kevin Bracken, was pulling up in his Suburban trying to gather his family to get them home. As he slowed down near the entrance doors he rolled down his window and shouted, "Hey Brent, you joining us for lunch?"

Brent almost answered in the affirmative, but then he remembered the commitment he made to his brother. "No, not today, sorry." Brent said.

Just then Jed's mom came out of the church. She saw Brent.

"You coming for lunch?" she asked.

"No, Mrs. Bracken, not today." Brent replied.

"You don't like my cooking, is that it?"

"No, no—that's not it at all."

"That's it; it's my cooking," she said with a big smile on her face as she climbed into the Suburban. Jed got in the back seat of the SUV.

"Make me a doggy bag," Brent shouted.

Brent wasn't sure what he was even doing. Mike would probably forget about the offer, and Brent would be stuck making lunch for himself. That meant cereal. He loved going to the

Brackens on Sunday afternoons. They had a great house on the shore of Lake Charlevoix. Plus, Jed's mom was an amazing cook. How could he improve on that offer? And now he was evading their invitations? For what?

Jed rolled down his window. "You guys coming tonight?" he called to Jackson and Brent.

"I'm coming. I'm going to bring my mom's old metal-wheel skates." Jackson said. "I'm going to tear it up!"

As the Suburban pulled away, Jed leaned out his window, "They won't even let you in."

"Oh, they'll let me in; they're paying me an appearance fee!" Jackson yelled as the car drove off.

"You're wearing your mom's skates? That's weird." Brent said.

"What? They fit me good." Jackson answered.

Even at 12:30 in the afternoon, the sun sat low on the horizon. The day was monochrome, light gray sky fading slightly into lighter gray snow. It was like the sky had just been desaturated of all its color, and now the world was presented only in black and white.

Jackson and Brent walked together along the street. They each lived close by. Jackson, who was naturally uncomfortable with silence, filled the space with words.

"It's hard to be this good lookin'. It's a constant struggle," he said.

"Uh huh," Brent answered.

"If you like, I could help you overcome your awkwardness with the ladies. All you have to do is ask."

"Jackson, the only reason girls hang around with you is because I'm friends with you," Brent said.

"That's possibly true. But your problem is you never know what to say to them. You need to win them over with words, seeing as you can't simply rely on good looks like I do. The key is to mention their eyes and their soul."

"Eyes and soul?" Brent said.

"Yeah, something like, 'Every time I look into your eyes, I feel like I can touch your soul,'" Jackson said.

"What?"

Brent heard the rumble of a loud throaty motorcycle coming in fast behind him. He didn't recognize the sound of the engine. It certainly wasn't his brother's Buell. The bike caught up to Brent and Jackson but instead of driving past them, it swerved to the side of the road, came to a stop, and cut them off from walking any further. There were two people on the bike.

The driver tore off his helmet. It was Mike. He turned around.

"Hey babe, could you get off and give the helmet to my brother?"

Melissa was Mike's sometimes girlfriend. She was momentarily confused. She took her helmet off revealing her jet black hair with a bright pink stripe down the side.

"What?" she asked with a healthy bite of anger in her voice.

"Just get off the bike, would ya; you can walk home from here," Mike said sarcastically. "I'm practically looking at your house. There's your dad." He waved. He was no where near her home.

"I'm not walking, and I'm not getting off this bike."

"Fine," Mike said. He abruptly gunned the throttle and popped a stationary wheelie. The jerky motion dumped Melissa right off the back of the bike. She would have fallen on her butt if Jackson hadn't caught her.

"What is wrong with you!" she hollered as she whipped her helmet into the snow bank.

"Hey, that's why we can't have nice things," Mike said. "Brent, would you please get on."

Brent was staring at the bike. It was a maroon and silver Harley-Davidson Fatboy.

"Where did you get this bike?" Brent asked.

"It was the prize at the spelling bee," Mike said. "Get on."

Brent hesitated a moment. He had promised to go with his brother, and to his surprise Mike had apparently remembered. Now Mike was dumping his girlfriend and giving him her seat. Brent was mildly flattered. He got on the bike. Jackson retrieved the helmet from the snow bank and handed it to Brent.

Mike yelled back to Melissa, "I'll call you."

"You will not!" she answered.

"That's true," Mike sneered as they drove off.

As the Harley roared away down the street, Jackson was left standing next to Melissa. He didn't consider this to be such a bad thing – she was kind of cute. He could adjust to the black and pink hair.

"Ah, chivalry," he said.

"He's such a jerk!" Melissa exclaimed as she stomped off down the street.

"You wanna talk about it?" Jackson asked, starting to chase after her.

"I'm not the one who needs counseling in this relationship. This former relationship!" she shouted at Mike.

Jackson saw an opportunity - a damsel in distress, his chance to comfort – maybe even charm her. He threw out his killer line.

"Hey, every time I look at your soul… it makes my eyes burn."

As soon as the words left his lips he realized he'd butchered his own line.

Melissa picked up her pace and didn't look back.

"Shut up, Jackson," he said to himself under his breath.

Brent hung on tight to his brother's leather jacket as they speed north on US-31. Brent wasn't dressed for a winter ride on the back of a motorcycle, and now he was absolutely freezing. Mike accelerated to over seventy miles per hour.

The frozen fields and smoking farmhouse chimneys flew by as Brent peeked out the side of his helmet. He tried to keep his head tucked behind Mike to minimize the wind.

There was no use trying to say anything; the bike was too loud. He wanted to ask where they were going, but he couldn't coordinate his frozen lips enough to even form a word.

After fifteen minutes, Mike finally slowed and turned down a small road that veered off the main road and wound through a forest of tall evergreens. The snow was deep back in these woods. Five minutes later Mike turned onto a long narrow driveway that wandered deeper into the forest. The long driveway had enough

bends and turns that Brent couldn't see the far end of it. It had been plowed recently, but the bike still struggled to maneuver through the packed snow base. Mike persisted, but eventually they had to get off the bike and push the Harley. Walking, they made a final turn and Brent saw where they were headed. At the end of the long snowy driveway was a big red barn.

"Wh-wh-where are we?" Brent's lips were too cold to form words correctly.

"It belongs to Frank's grandfather Mike answered. "He's too old to know he's senile, so nobody knows we're out here."

CHAPTER TWELVE

INSIDE THE BARN SEAN'S MAKESHIFT gang had the meth lab nearly operational. Frank was moving all over the place, jabbering, and generally not helping anybody do anything. He was waving a copy of the Sunday newspaper's sports section in his hand, showing it to anyone who would listen. The front page featured a big picture of T.J. Lewis and the headline, "Lewis Leads Rayders Again."

Frank pointed the picture out to Big Mack. "See this kid, this kid right here?" Frank said, pointing to the picture of T.J. "He pulled a knife on me last night."

Big Mack wasn't buying it. "And that's why you came back empty-handed," He said sarcastically.

Frank wouldn't let it go. "I wasn't goin' after much, but I was halfway out the door, heck, I was all the way out the door. It was a done deal, and then this high school punk pulls a knife on me," Frank lied.

"Why?" Big Mack asked, as he kept working.

"How should I know? That's just what they do," Frank said. "Anyway, I just hauled off and cracked him in the face, and then he, you know, dropped the knife."

"And that's when you dropped the... what was it you were liftin' again?"

"CD's, I was liftin' CD's," Frank replied.

"What are we going to do with those?" Big Mack said, laughing out loud.

"Sell them, you idiot," Frank said. "People buy CD's. You have CD's; you bought them didn't you?"

Mike opened the large sliding doors to the Barn and pushed Brent through the entrance. Brent was thrilled to feel any heat, and the first thing he noticed was a small fire stove burning in the corner. The next thing he noticed was the smell. It was rancid, like a mixture of finger nail polish and dog piss. As soon as Mike and Brent entered the barn, Frank walked straight up to them. He was still pointing at T.J.'s picture in the paper.

"Hey there, you know this kid, the big star?" Frank asked while shoving the picture toward Brent.

"Of course I know him." Brent said.

"You know he pulled a knife on me last night."

"What are you talking about?" Brent asked.

"Everyone thinks this kid is fifteen-years-old, but he's like twenty-one; that's why he's so good," Frank said. "I checked him out."

"That's bull. You're an idiot," Brent said.

"Admit it. Haven't you wondered why we have a black preacher in this town and why his kid is everybody's All-American?"

Brent just rolled his eyes, "Mike…"

"Frank! Please." A short man with a black leather jacket, an Irish bowler hat, and a deep Dublin accent walked out from the shadows. Brent could tell from his tone that he was the guy in charge. Frank instantly deferred to the hat's authority and slinked away without a fuss.

"Hello Brent." The man in the hat was calm. "Don't mind Frank. He's just upset that your black friend pulled a knife on him." Sean continued.

"That would upset anybody," Frank shouted from the other side of the barn.

"What knife?" Brent asked.

"And he wants to be sure that kind of thing doesn't happen again. It's just about respect." Sean said.

"There was no knife." Brent stated matter-of-factly. He knew T.J. and he knew T.J. wouldn't pull a knife on anybody.

"Well anyway—thanks for comin' out. My name is Sean. I guess you're here because your big brother sees some potential in you."

Brent hadn't expected this. Mike had spoken well of him? Mike saw potential in him? Brent couldn't remember his big brother saying anything nice to him or about him for as long as he'd been alive.

"Potential for what?" Brent asked sincerely.

"Well that's just the thing. Potential for what?" Sean pulled a one hundred-dollar bill out of his coat pocket, grabbed Brent's hand, and placed it in his fist.

Brent looked down at the bill. It seemed to be real! It was crisp and stiff. He'd never held a hundred dollar bill before in his life.

"I may have a role for you, if you can be trusted," Sean said.

"Trusted for what?"

Sean put his arm around Brent and led him away from Mike. He wanted to talk to Brent in private. He spoke quietly. "I want you to join us. We need someone on the inside of the high school. You'll be well paid, and you'll make your brother proud."

Brent still did not know what Sean was asking of him. Getting paid well sounded good, but in exchange for what exactly?

"I'm not doing anything illegal, and I'm not selling any drugs," Brent said.

"Brent, don't make a hasty decision here."

Sean led Brent to an old wooden bench on the far side of the barn. He motioned for Brent to sit. Sean leaned in as if he was telling him a private secret. He spoke softly.

"Your future is at stake now. At least do me the favor of thinking it over." Sean handed another hundred-dollar bill to Brent.

Brent accepted what was now his second hundred-dollar bill. He had two hundred bucks in his pocket! That was by far the most pocket change he had ever had at one time, a far cry from the three singles Jed's dad gave him.

"Think about it. Sit here and think about it." Sean said. "Would you like a beer?"

Brent paused and then looked up at Sean.

"What do you want from me?"

Sean looked him straight in the eye, straightened his cap, and said simply, "Loyalty."

CHAPTER THIRTEEN

The fire stove was on the far end of the barn, and the temperature outside was dropping rapidly. The warmth from that far wasn't doing a thing for the air where Brent sat. And while Brent sat in a dark cold barn thinking about his future, Jed was lying on the couch in his own warm living room watching a Red Wings game with his dad. Brent was cold and hungry. Jed was warm and well fed.

Jed usually held a basketball when he watched television. He had the ball in his right hand, tortilla chips in his left.

"You've got some skate tournament tonight?" his dad asked.

Jed laughed. "Tournament?"

Jed's dad smacked him with his newspaper. "You know what I mean, whatever, at the rink, tonight?"

"It's not really a tournament, it's just a youth group event."

Jed's mom walked into the living room with a fresh bowl of guacamole.

"You guys good?" she asked as she put the bowl on the coffee table.

"Good?" Jed's dad answered. "We're watching hockey, you're in the kitchen cookin', the house is warm... how could life get any better than this?"

Jed's mom plopped down on the couch. "You know, Jed," she said, "it was your dad's sophistication that first drew me to him."

Jed laughed.

"Thank you, darling," Jed's dad said. He gave her a kiss on the cheek. Then, as if to prove his "sophistication," he let out a belly-deep belch that echoed through the living room. With a big grin on his face, he looked at Jed and whispered, "She loves me!"

Inside the barn, Brent pulled his watch out—4:03. The afternoon was getting late, and his feet were practically numb. None of the heat was reaching him. He couldn't say yes to something he didn't understand, but he was reluctant to say no to a guy who had just forked over two hundred bucks.

Brent got up and shuffled toward Mike. Mike pulled a swig from his beer.

"You in?" Mike asked his brother.

Brent hesitated. "Can we just go home now?"

Mike just glared at him. "Don't you make me look stupid for bringing you out here."

Brent turned around and went back to his bench.

Jed's house had a great view of Lake Charlevoix. By 4:15 the sun was low in the sky, and the ice glistened across the frozen lake. Despite the beauty, Jed wasn't looking at the lake; the hockey game was going to overtime.

When the Red Wings game went to commercial, Jed hit the mute button on the television. The commercials were always louder than the game itself. In the momentary silence, Jed's dad resumed his inquiry.

"So this tournament tonight, this "not" tournament. Are there any prizes?"

"Well, I think the winner gets to stay after and help Butch clean up," Jed answered.

"To the victor goes the soils," Mr. Bracken said.

From the kitchen Jed's mom cried out with a sigh, "I heard that!"

Jed un-muted the television and shook his head. "That's pretty bad dad," he said.

:]

By 5:30 it was completely dark outside. The barn was colder than ever, and Brent was eager to go.

Sean walked over toward Brent, pulled up a chair, and put one foot on the seat. He studied Brent. "So, I hear you're in a gang?" Sean said.

"No," said Brent.

"So what's the Frontier Boys?"

Brent laughed. "Not a gang. Just a name."

"What's the story?"

Brent shook his head, confused.

"Hey, you got a name, you gotta have a story." Sean said.

"It's nothin'," Brent said. "We were ten years old—just boys. We caught some fish down off the pier. Salmon. Jackson decides we could sell 'em, so we kind of just carried 'em downtown to Bucky's place. Thought he'd pay us some money, but, you know, the fish kind of fell all over the floor and stuff. And it would have been nothin', but there was this guy from the newspaper there. He took this picture and wrote this story, called us the modern Frontier Boys. That's it. It's no gang. We never even got paid for the fish."

Sean smiled and said, "With me you can make some real money. No fish."

:]

The Lewis' lived in a small two-story house on a wooded lot just down the street from the church. Sunday afternoons were sacred nap times for Rev. Lewis.

While his dad napped, T.J. was in his room carrying on an overseas internet chat with a friend he met in Ghana the previous summer. For three weeks T.J. had worked with a mission organization digging water wells in rural African villages. Prosper was the Christian name of the young Ghanaian man who organized the efforts. T.J. had never met anyone in his life who worked harder, or who had a bigger smile. Prosper had a joyful disposition that never quit, and his tireless work ethic blew T.J.'s mind. Every Sunday afternoon T.J. got in touch with Prosper on-line.

"Whatcha doin'?" Jordyn asked as she walked into T.J.'s room.

"I'm socially networking," T.J. answered.

"Who you talkin' to?" Jordyn asked.

"Prosper. I met him at the mission school in Ghana."

"What are you talkin' about?" Jordyn asked.

"God mostly," T.J. answered. "And soccer."

Jordyn looked over T.J.'s shoulder and followed the thread of the conversation.

"Here, can I talk to him?" she asked as she bumped T.J. out of the way.

"Sure," T.J. said. He let her slide in front of the computer. He grabbed a NERF ball and took a shot at the hoop he had mounted on his bedroom door.

"I want to find out what you were really up to last summer," Jordyn said playfully.

"You should go there. You would love it," T.J. said. "When we dedicated that well the people danced for two days. One well saved the women a daily walk of eleven miles each way just to get water."

"Why do the women carry the water? What are the men doing?" Jordyn asked.

"Good question." T.J. answered. "When you go there you can ask them."

Jordyn really was amazed by her little brother. He cared for other people, and his faith in God led him to action. If he was impressed with a guy like Prosper, then Prosper must indeed be a pretty impressive guy.

A few blocks away at the Bracken house Jed and his dad were in the kitchen washing dishes.

"What's Brent up to today? Why didn't he join us?" Mr. Bracken asked, with his hands in the soapy dishwater.

"I don't know," Jed answered as he toweled off a wet plate.

"His mom works on Sunday, doesn't she? It's not like that boy to miss a free meal."

Jed paused. "Maybe he's doing homework."

"Yeah right!" said his dad, and both of them cracked up.

Brent was definitely not doing homework. At that moment he was sitting on a hard wooden bench in a dark smelly barn freezing his rear end off and starving. He did, however, have two hundred dollars in his pocket. He wondered if he would have to give them back if he didn't agree to Sean's terms of engagement – whatever those were. Maybe Sean was so rich he'd already forgotten about the money.

Mike was having misgivings about bringing Brent out in the first place. For one thing, he didn't really trust Brent to keep his mouth shut about what was going on. Brent could be a talker. For another, there was the slightest touch of protectiveness somewhere in him, and he knew he was potentially involving his little brother in something dangerous. He walked over near the fire stove and talked to Sean.

"I don't think this is going to work for him." Mike said.

"It'll work. Everybody takes the money in the end." Sean said.

"Why would you want him anyway?" Mike asked.

"He's in high school. What better dealer for a high-schooler than one of their own?" Sean answered.

Mike looked over at Brent. "He's not..."

"Put him in the car," Sean said.

"Why."

"Put him in the game." Sean said.

CHAPTER FOURTEEN

AT 6:45 IN THE EVENING, Brent finally left the barn. They were going for a drive, and he found himself being shoved next to Frank in the backseat of a classic two-door 1968 candy apple green Chevy Camaro. Sean was driving, Mike riding shotgun. The 357 rear-wheel-drive engine was well suited for summertime street racing, but horribly ill equipped for riding on January snow covered roads. The Camaro zig-zagged out the driveway and fish-tailed its way around the steep turns of Indian Trails Road. Brent had no idea where they were going, but he was at least glad to be out of the freezing barn.

"Time to go visit your black friend. We have something for him," Frank said.

The more Frank talked the less Brent liked him. Frank said nonsensical things; he obviously lied as often as he told the truth. Brent wondered why was he so obsessed with T.J.?

"What? What do you have for him?" Brent asked.

"Oh, you'll see." Frank said, snickering.

"Why, what do you have for him?" Brent persisted.

"A message!" Sean answered from the front seat. His tone of voice was as firm as the grip he had on the steering wheel. "Just tell me where I'm going."

"I have no idea where you're going," Brent said.

"I just told you, we're going to visit your little black friend," Frank said.

What did Sean mean that he had a "message" for T.J.? He wasn't sure what they were asking of him. On one hand, Brent didn't want to tell them anything about T.J. On the other hand, he wanted to go to the skating rink himself, he knew T.J. would be there, and he wanted to get away from Frank.

"Why don't you just drop me off at the skating rink, and I'll tell him myself."

"No, we'll tell him," Frank giggled.

"The skating rink," Sean smiled. "Now Michael, which way is the skating rink?"

The Camaro sped off down the cold dark highway.

Jed, T.J., and around twenty other kids from the church were standing outside the Flight Deck Skating Rink just south of town. They were waiting for Butch to show up with the keys to the building. The Flight Deck was normally open only a few months of the year. January wasn't one of those months, but Butch was able to finagle the keys from the owners. The keys he'd accidentally left by the sink in his trailer.

It was a cold night, and the kids were bundled up in coats, hats, and scarves while they waited for Butch to return with the keys. Jed and T.J. were wearing their letter jackets. Brent was nowhere in sight.

Jackson got dropped off by his mom. "Hey guys. Why are we standing around outside in the cold instead of skating little circles in the warm inside?" Jackson asked.

"We're locked out. Butch forgot the keys," T.J. said.

"You bring your mom's skates?" Jed asked.

"Nope." Jackson answered. "I don't need skates to go skating. I'm that good."

:]

Inside the Camaro the music was blaring. Sean was driving well over the speed limit as he came through the heart of downtown.

"You want to lead these boys?" Sean said to Mike in his fatherly tone. "You want to lead them? Well, this is how you do it." He reached into his leather coat and pulled a Glock 19 semi-automatic 9mm pistol.

"Nobody, nobody messes with your boys. That's how you lead. It's better to be feared than loved."

Brent couldn't see what was happening in the front seat.

Sean handed Mike the gun, "Send the message."

Sean pulled a black knit neck warmer up over his face. Mike did the same. Mike rolled the window down and the Camaro angled toward the skating rink with the crowd of kids standing outside. Then Brent saw the gun.

"Mike, what are you doing with a gun?" Brent cried out.

"That's him," Frank shouted as he pointed toward T.J.

Sean hit the gas, and the Camaro responded with a roar. "Aim high," Sean said as he accelerated toward the rink.

Glock in hand, Mike extended his right arm out the window.

"Mike, Mike! No!" Brent screamed.

Brent reached forward in desperation and grabbed Mike's arm. Just as Brent's hands reached Mike's arm, the gun fired.

BAM! ... BAM! BAM! Three quick shots rang out with incredible volume and instantly shocked the group of kids outside the rink. Everyone flinched. The roaring engine of the green Camaro sped away as screams of pandemonium rang outside the rink.

Brent didn't see what had happened. Frank pulled Brent down into the backseat as the car sped away from the scene. Had Mike really just shot bullets into a group of innocent kids? Did he hit anybody? Brent didn't know, and neither did anyone else in the car.

"Oh man, nice shootin' Lee Harvey, nice shootin'!" Frank was giddy. "They scattered like cockroaches runnin' from the light. Nice shootin', Mikey. You made my whole day!"

Brent was physically shaking and not because he was cold. Surely Mike had fired high, hadn't he? But he had grabbed Mike's arm. He had pulled it down just before the shots rang out.

CHAPTER FIFTEEN

Sean drove the speed limit all the way back to Indian Trails Road. He pulled up to the barn and brought the car right inside. The Camaro could be identified, and now would have to go into deep storage until it could be repainted or chopped. He didn't care. The car belonged to Frank's grandfather, and Frank's grandfather had long ago forgotten what day it was. The guys in the barn were still cooking. They had no idea what had just taken place. Frank couldn't wait to tell them.

"That'll scare 'em," said Frank, as soon as he climbed out of the car. Brent stayed in the back seat, unable to move.

Sean saw the confusion and worry in Brent's face, and he wasted no time making things clear. As soon as the engine was off he walked around the car, reached into the back seat, and grabbed Brent's collar, pulling his face upward.

"Nobody ever shot a gun tonight," Sean whispered, just inches from Brent's face. "Anyone asks—you were home watching television. Figure out what was on. Understand?"

Brent was numb. He stared back blankly, and Sean leaned in so close that that their noses almost touched.

"And if you ever, ever say anything about this to anybody—your mommy gets hurt."

Brent's eyes went to the floor. Sean relaxed his grip and backed up. He even smiled a little.

"Oh, and hey, Brent, by the way, you're in." Sean walked away.

Brent fell back into the seat. Brent had never really prayed much in his life, but suddenly he was begging God, "Please, God. Please, God. Let everyone be okay." If there was a God, and He could hear the prayers that Brent was saying, then maybe that God would help. On the other hand, if there was a God, then that God would have seen everything that just happened. The way Brent figured, he had just betrayed his friend for two hundred bucks. What God would ever overlook something like that?

Mike, Sean, and the rest of the guys in the barn had two cases of beer they were intent upon getting through in celebration of their successful evening. Brent stayed in the back seat of the Camaro, trying to convince himself that the shots had missed everybody, and everyone was fine, and that since no real harm had been done, God would probably forgive him. But if those bullets had hit anybody—he didn't even want to consider that possibility. So he just kept praying. "Please God, let everybody be okay..."

By 1:30 in the morning Mike decided to borrow a pick up truck, and despite the beer in his system, drive home to his own bed. Brent was surprised when he walked into the living room and saw his mom sleeping on the couch, still fully dressed. The television was on, as were the lights. A half full bottle of tequila and empty glass sat on the side table.

She stirred when she heard the boys come in the door.

"What time is it? Where have you guys been? Thank God you're okay. Have you heard the news?" She yawned and rubbed her eyes.

"What news?" Brent asked.

"Oh, honey—I don't even want to tell you."

"Mom, what happened?"

"Your friend, T.J. Lewis—he got shot. Somebody just drove up in their car and shot him."

Brent felt his heart stop and his breath escape. His eyes fell slowly to the floor. He didn't know how to process those words, so he said nothing.

"They drove him off in the ambulance. It was on the news. I thought you were with him, but I talked to Jed's mom, and she said that Jed hadn't seen you all night long. Then you didn't come home, and I got worried. I was waiting up for you, or at least I tried to—I guess I dozed off. I thought you might want to go down there, to the hospital."

Brent felt a cold chill creep right down his spine into his shoes. His toes felt like they were frozen to the floor. Mike was standing right next to him, watching Brent's reaction.

"You guys go," Mike said, "He doesn't really know me." Mike glanced back at Brent and walked toward the hallway. There was a rare hint of fear on his face.

"And Brent, thanks for being a good little brother."

CHAPTER SIXTEEN

EVEN AT QUARTER AFTER TWO in the morning the waiting room at the Charlevoix Hospital was filled with people who were concerned about T.J. Jed's mother and father were there, along with Jackson, Jed, Butch, and most of the kids from the rink, some of whom were sleeping on the floor.

A little more than seven hours prior the unsuspecting teens had scattered when the sound of the gunshots rang out from the mysterious car. Within minutes the parking lot was illuminated with the emergency lights of police, fire, and medical vehicles. Paramedics carefully lifted T.J. onto a gurney and gently placed him in the back of the ambulance. Everybody knew T.J., and everybody liked him. To see him lying bloody and unconscious in the middle of the parking lot was an incomprehensible shock.

Students had gathered together in groups of two and three and began to pray and cry out to the Lord. Many of them had never prayed so fervently or sincerely in their entire lives.

Jordyn Lewis was dozing on a yellow couch in the waiting area, but Reverend Lewis was not asleep. When Brent came running through the corridor and into the waiting room, Reverend Lewis looked up.

"Brent," he said.

"What happened?" Brent was panting.

"You don't know?"

"My mom said T.J. got shot."

Ms. Fencett followed Brent into the room.

"Hello Lois. Thanks for coming. Can I get you some coffee?" Reverend Lewis offered.

"Um, sure, please."

Jed was sitting on a couch. He looked up at Brent.

"Where have you been?" he asked.

"Nowhere, at home—watching television," Brent lied as he sat down next to Jed.

Reverend Lewis brought a cup of coffee for Brent's mom, then turned to Brent. "There was a drive-by shooting tonight outside the skating rink. Three shots were fired." Reverend Lewis stopped abruptly. He could barely choke out the words.

"We think the bullets hit the concrete wall. One of them ricocheted off the wall and..." He stopped again. He had to swallow air for a second before his voice would continue. "One of them is currently lodged in the lower portion of T.J.'s spine."

"What does that mean? I mean, how is he? Is he going to be okay?" Brent cried.

"He's lost a lot of blood. You know how unpredictable spinal cord injuries are. And plus, he hit his head. He's been unconscious since. Right now he's in surgery."

"But is he gonna be alright?" Brent asked.

"We're praying," said Reverend Lewis. "We're praying, and we're hoping."

Brent was shaking again. He didn't know where to look or what to do with his hands. His wanted to crumple on the floor. "Oh God, God, God…" He couldn't bear the news. He had to leave. He stood up and ran out of the room.

Reverend Lewis had been holding himself together, but suddenly he felt the pent up anger in him bubbling forth. The former boxer was a gentle man, a pastor in every sense of the word. But once he had known violence, once he was a fighter. Suddenly the fighter in him wanted a chance to speak. He pounded his massive fist into his hand and cried out, "Who would shoot at a child? Who? I'll kill 'em!"

Jed's dad rushed over to Reverend Lewis. "Hey, c'mon now. C'mon. That's not going to do T.J. any good."

Suddenly all Rev. Lewis could see was the senseless cowardice of a thug with a gun, shooting and gunning down his beautiful son. Rev. Lewis had once grieved the loss of his wife to cancer. The thought of losing his only son was suddenly more than he could contain.

"I'll kill 'em! I'll kill 'em! I swear to God, I'll kill 'em!" Reverend Lewis was shouting and shaking Jed's dad around like a rag doll.

Kevin Bracken was not a small man, he stood about six foot five, and he put his hands on Rev. Lewis' shoulders to try and calm him down. Kevin Bracken hung on for dear life as Reverend Lewis' anger roared out of the furnace of his broken heart. In a few moments though the hot rage was replaced by overwhelming grief. The big reverend nearly collapsed. Wails of sorrow burst uncontrollably from deep within him.

In the hallway outside the waiting room, Brent felt like he was about to explode. He had heard the whole thing. He burst out the

front doors of the hospital and sprinted across the parking lot as fast as he could run. He kept moving his feet, running away from the hospital, running away from his friends. But he could not run away from his guilty conscience. That followed him as he ran and ran. When he finally stopped running the first rays of sunlight were beginning to filter over the midnight blue horizon.

CHAPTER SEVENTEEN

MONDAY WAS A SCHOOL DAY, but nobody at Charlevoix High felt like going. The entire faculty was in shock. Drive by shootings didn't happen in quiet little northern towns. The students walked like zombies thought the hallways.

Mr. Klein, the principal, called an assembly first thing in the morning. The students dutifully filed into the auditorium, sat down, and stared ahead at the curtain. No one was talking. The principal finally took the microphone.

"By now most of you have heard about the terrible tragedy that happened last night. One of our students, T.J. Lewis, was seriously wounded in a drive-by shooting." He paused, visibly shaken by what he was trying to say to the kids.

"Someone fired a gun from a moving car. T.J. was struck in the spine by a fragment of the bullet. This morning I stopped by the hospital. I regret to inform you that T.J. has not regained consciousness, nor has he moved a muscle since being struck. He is listed in critical condition. They are keeping him alive right now using respirators and heart stimulation, but as of this morning anyway, there were no independent signs of brain activity. I will not pretend to have an explanation or an answer for why this

93

happened. This was a senseless and cowardly act of violence. I don't know what else to say."

Mr. Klein stopped and looked at the hundreds of silent students in front of him. From near the back of the auditorium a hand went up. It was Jordyn Lewis. Mr. Klein immediately recognized her as T.J.'s sister and tried to give her a smile.

"Yes?" he asked.

Jordyn had to yell a bit in order for the principal to hear her.

"Could we pray?" she called out.

Mr. Klein glanced uncomfortably at a couple of the teachers around him. He clearly noticed a firm shake of several heads.

"No, Jordyn, I'm sorry. That would not be appropriate for this setting."

Jordyn's best friend, Lara, put her arm around her.

"We may, I suppose, observe a moment of silence," Mr. Klein said.

A thick silence filled the room. Some students began praying anyway, appropriate or not. Others just looked straight ahead, unsure of what to do. Jed was praying, Jackson was looking around to see how other students were reacting. Brent was not at school that day.

CHAPTER EIGHTEEN

A WEEK PASSED. IT WAS SATURDAY afternoon when Brent finally decided to come out of his room. He called Jed's house. Mrs. Bracken answered the phone.

"Brent, how are you doing?"

"I've been better," Brent answered. "Is Jed around?"

"He's out on the ice; he's fishing. You should go out to see him. I think he could use the company."

"Okay."

"You know where Kevin's shanty is?"

"I can find it."

It was a bright blue-sky day, and Lake Charlevoix was frozen and covered with fresh white snow. Fishing shanties tend to group together in small communities in various locations on the massive expanse of the seventeen-mile-long lake. Jed's dad had a red shanty grouped within in a small impromptu village of the little cabins not far from the western shore. Jed liked the quiet of the shanty, especially in these days. He was confused and hurting.

He realized it could have easily been him who was hit with that bullet, but felt guilty for even thinking that way. His best friend was still lying unconscious, and he didn't know what to do. So he brought his pocket Bible with him into the shanty, lit the small wood stove in the corner, dropped a line into the black water, and opened the book.

Brent stepped out on the ice and headed toward the distant village of shanties on the horizon. As he trudged step by step through the deep snow he wondered what he was going to say to Jed. He wanted to tell him exactly what had happened. He was caught in no man's land, but he kept walking toward the only shanty with smoke rising from its metal chimney. After fifteen minutes of walking he reached the small red wooden hut. He almost turned around—but he didn't.

He knocked on the tiny window along the back wall. Jed looked up, smiled, and waved him in. Brent walked around to the front of the shanty and opened the door. Jed squinted as the bright light from the outside hit his face.

"Where have you been?" Jed asked.

"Nowhere."

"You have to go to school, you know."

"I know. I will," Brent said.

"C'mon in. Grab a bucket."

Jed kept one hand on his fishing pole and flipped over an extra bucket. There was barely room for two people inside the small plywood structure. When the door closed the ambient light came partly from the small window, but mostly from the ice itself. There were two holes cut in the ice. The day was so bright outside that the ice glowed as if it was fluorescent. Jed's fishing line had a blue bobber floating atop the coal black water. Brent sat down on the bucket and stared at the bobber. Finally, he spoke.

"Any news?" Brent asked.

"No."

They sat in silence for a good long while.

Jed stared into the water. The bobber was almost perfectly still.

"Jed, do you believe in life after death?" Brent asked.

"I believe in God," Jed answered.

"Is that the same thing?"

Jed paused and looked up at his friend. Brent was obviously deeply troubled.

"Well, I was literally just reading," Jed said, as he pulled his Bible out of the front left pocket of his letter jacket. "Jesus was talking to, well, some people, and He said, 'Whoever hears My word, and believes Him who sent Me, has eternal life.'"

Brent sat still for a moment, pondering those words, the promise of life after death for believers. He wanted to find comfort in them, but he could not. He looked up and said, "Well, that's kind of hard to believe when T.J. is lying in a hospital bed with tubes keeping him alive."

Jed paused, closed the Bible, and put it back in his pocket.

"Yeah, I miss him, too."

They sat for a long while, thinking about their friend. The shanty was a cocoon of protection from the harsh elements. As they sat in silence they could hear the howl of the winds picking up outside. The layer of ice they were sitting on was a twelve-inch

barrier of protection keeping them from the deep and chilling waters of Lake Charlevoix. The line between life and death was razor thin, but it was a line that teenage boys seldom considered.

Brent was taking this especially hard. He had locked himself in his room for a week. Jed tried to think of something he could do to help his friend. Finally, he handed his fishing pole to Brent.

"Here, hold this," Jed said, and he got up and walked out of the shanty.

Once outside, he grabbed his cell phone and called Jackson.

Jackson was at the hospital. He stopped by hoping to find out something, anything, about T.J. But there was nothing to find out. Jackson looked through the open blinds of the window to T.J.'s room and saw his friend lying motionless on the bed. There were tubes running into him, machines hooked up to him. He felt his cell phone buzz, and he saw Jed calling. He stepped outside to answer.

"Jackson, where are you?

"I'm at the hospital. Where are you?"

"I'm out on the lake," Jed replied. "I've got an idea. I think there's something that we could do, and it would be good to get Brent moving again."

"Go on," Jackson said.

"Okay, well, let's try to find the guys who did this; let's find the shooters ourselves," Jed said.

"Might I remind you that's why we have the po-lice. They've got private eyes, Jack Bauer, James Bond…"

"Yeah," Jed interrupted, "but maybe we can help."

"Okay, tell you what. You go help the cops, and I'll stay here and see what I can do to assist the brain surgeons."

Just then Brent yelled from inside the shanty, "Hey Jed, you've got a fish!"

"Reel him in," Jed yelled back to Brent.

Brent grabbed the pole and fought what seemed to be a fantastic sized fish. For a moment Brent forgot about being depressed and focused on nothing but getting that fish up and through the cut in the ice. The short pole bent in half, and Brent fought a battle with whatever fish was just below the surface.

Standing outside the shanty Jed was oblivious to the fish war Brent was waging. "Just meet me and Brent at my house," Jed said to Jackson. "Let's see if we can find that car."

Moments later Brent came out the door of the shanty carrying a beautiful thirty-inch Northern Pike still on the line. Jed was impressed.

"Bring him along Frontier Boy. We've got to go!" Jed said, as he started running toward the western shore.

CHAPTER NINETEEN

JED JOGGED ACROSS THE ICE, up onto the shore, and into his garage. Brent kept right with him, still carrying the Northern Pike.

"Hey, what do you want me to do with this?" Brent asked, holding up the fish.

"Just throw him in the snow bank," Jed said, as he scrambled into the house and up the stairs to his room.

Brent tossed the fish next to the house and kicked some extra snow over the top of him. He'd stay frozen until they had time to clean him.

Jed was ready to start hunting, and his prey was the shooters car. He had caught a brief glimpse of the car the night of the shooting. If there was one thing Jed knew well, it was cars. He pegged the car as a late '60s Chevy Camaro, and he was also pretty sure it had been some shade of green. As soon as Jed made it upstairs to his room, he began shedding his boots, snow pants, hat, and jacket.

Shortly after, Brent came running up the stairs and into Jed's room.

"You know that car that the shooters were in?" He asked Brent.

"No, I wasn't there," Brent answered.

"Well, I'm pretty sure it was a Camaro, late '60s. It was dark, but I think it was green."

"Well, you would know," Brent said. After all, Brent had seen Jed identify cars by nothing but their headlight patterns.

Jed reached into a box in his closet and grabbed a stack of magazines called *Wheels and Keels. Wheels and Keels* was full of photographs of cars and boats listed for sale within about a four county region. Jed had collected them for years in anticipation of one day buying his first car. Jed plopped a handful of the magazines into Brent's hands.

"*Wheels and Keels*? What do you want me to do with these?"

"What can it hurt? Maybe we'll get lucky. Start lookin'," Jed said.

"For what?" Brent said.

"For the car, for the Camaro. If it's ever been sold around here, maybe it's in the magazine. Maybe we can find out who sold it, and then maybe we could find out who bought it."

Brent hesitated. Actually, he didn't want to get anywhere close to finding the green Camaro. "Why don't you just check the website?" he said. It was the first thing that popped into his brain.

Jed paused and looked up, "Good idea," he said.

Jed went to his desk and opened his laptop. He did a search for *Wheels and Keels*. When the homepage came up, he typed in "Chevy Camaro," and entered a search radius of 100 miles. He waited impatiently while it searched its database for hits. While he waited, Jed opened another tab to check his Facebook page. He saw he had a message—a message from T.J. Impossible – unless…

"Brent check this out, I just got a message from T.J.!" Jed couldn't believe it.

"What?"

"Listen to this," Jed scanned the message quickly, then read it out loud:

> *I am surrounded by the most beautiful people I have ever seen. With one glance I love them. It is so sudden, so different from any feeling I have had before. God is so real here.*

"Do you think this means he's all right?" Brent asked.

Jed didn't know what to say. Just then he heard the garage door opening. "That's my dad," he said as he ran out of his room and down the stairs.

Jed's dad was pulling into the driveway in his big Chevy Suburban as Jed ran out to meet the car. He threw his hands on the hood and launched his feet in the air. He was full of excitement and energy. The Suburban stopped and Jed scooted over to the driver's window.

"Dad, I just got a message from T.J!"

"Yeah?"

"Let's go to the hospital."

"Let's check," Mr. Bracken said, and he pulled out his cell phone.

Jed was so excited he couldn't stand still. He rocked the car as he stood on the sideboards while his dad dialed the phone.

Reverend Lewis was standing in his son's hospital room when he felt his cell phone vibrate in his pocket. He answered, "Hello."

"Reverend Lewis? Kevin Bracken calling. How's T.J.?"

Reverend Lewis looked down at his son lying in the hospital bed. T.J. was only breathing because of the respirator tube that was shoved down his throat. He had wires attached to his head. He hadn't moved or even blinked since he was first admitted.

"The same. Keep praying," Reverend Lewis answered softly.

"Okay, let me do it right now," Mr. Bracken answered.

"We're still here, God; we're still asking. Take T.J. by the hand like you took Jairus' daughter 2000 years ago. Bring him back like you brought her back."

Jed was confused and shook his head, "He's not better?"

"Not yet, Son, not yet."

This made no sense.

CHAPTER TWENTY

JED'S DAD PULLED INTO THE garage as Jed stood in the middle of the driveway.

"I don't get it. He just wrote me," he said to himself.

Brent came out of the house just as Jackson's mom drove into the driveway in her gold minivan. Brent picked up a basketball from the garage and dribbled it out towards Jed.

"Thanks, Mom," Jackson said as he climbed out of the minivan. "What'd I miss?"

Jed ignored the question, "C'mon, let's go."

He headed back into the house, back to his computer to continue his search. Jackson and Brent followed. Jed quickly realized that the computer wasn't going to be of help, and he closed his laptop. "The website is no good," he said. "They only show what is for sale today. We need to go back in time."

"Great idea, Jed—time travel. Glad I came," Jackson said.

"Not time travel; research. You saw the car; start looking."

Jed explained his idea to Jackson and divided the labor. His plan was to search through every single *Wheels and Keels* magazine he'd collected since he was seven years old in hopes of tracking down the shooter's car. He planned to make a list of every late 60's Camaro, call every seller, and learn whatever he could about what happened to the car.

Brent plopped down on Jed's bed, less than enthusiastic about the plan.

Jed tossed Jackson a handful of old *Wheels and Keels* magazines.

"Look for the car? I don't know anything about cars. I don't even know what kind of car my mom drives," Jackson said.

Brent wasn't interested. "Jed, have you lost your mind?" he asked. "You really think we're going to find the car in all of this?" Brent pointed to the stacks of magazines Jed was pulling out from his closet.

"Why not? I've got millions of these things. We just find out everyone who sold late '60s Camaros, we call 'em up, and we find out who they sold 'em to," Jed said.

"Camaros, got it," Jackson said. "What's a Camaro look like again?"

Jed's love of sports and cars was displayed all over his room. Posters, sports equipment, certificates, trophies, and rows of model cars all revealed Jed's interests. It was easy for Jed to show Jackson what a Camaro looked like: he grabbed a model from his dresser and tossed it to him.

"Like this," Jed said.

For the next two and a half hours Jed, Brent, and Jackson went through page after page of old issues. Jed was thorough, focused, and fast. He kept a stack of index cards on his knee and wrote down every possible option. Jackson was quiet, unusual for him, and intense. His mouth only moved when he saw something promising. Brent turned the pages slowly. He didn't actually look at them. He wasn't actually trying.

Finally, Jed found a hit.

"Bingo," Jed said. "It's perfect. And it's a local number."

He circled the picture of a green Camaro. The caption read:

> 1968 Chevy Camaro. 88,000 miles. 340 ci engine. Runs good, new shocks, cassette stereo, good tires. Asking $4200. Call (231) 555-2509. Ask for Earl.

Brent stared at the picture in the magazine, shocked. It looked just like the car he'd been in.

"Jed, this is crazy. That issue is six years old, you can't…"

Jed tossed Brent his cell phone.

"Dial this number," Jed said, dictating the number from the page.

Brent shook his head, but punched in the number. The phone rang and a voice answered, "Hello, this is Earl." Brent had no idea what to do.

"Talk to him," Jed said.

Brent froze with a blank stare on his face. "What?" he said.

"Give me the phone."

Brent tossed Jed the cell phone. "Hello, this is Jed."

Jed walked out of the room. In Brent's mind the only thing worse than *looking* for the car the shooters had used would be actually *finding* the car. He remembered Sean's words all too well, and he had no doubt that Sean was serious. If Sean found out Brent was snooping around or leading anyone to his operation Brent seriously worried for his own safety, not to mention his mom's.

Jackson had no such misgivings, and he actually found the private detective work sort of stimulating. He also assumed he would be exceptionally good at it. After Jed left the room he pulled his mirrored aviator sunglasses out of his pocket, put them on, looked at Brent and deadpanned, "CSI, Charlevoix."

Brent almost smiled.

Jed moved to the driveway to finish his conversation with Earl. By now it was dark outside. A floodlight on the house lit up the driveway basketball court. Brent and Jackson emerged just as Jed hung up the phone. Brent tossed him the basketball.

"What'd he say?" Brent asked.

"Said he couldn't tell me anything," Jed said as he shot the ball.

Brent grabbed the ball as it came through the hoop.

"So it's a dead end?" Brent asked.

"So, we're going to see him tomorrow," Jed said with a big smile.

Brent tossed the ball to Jackson, who was standing at the free throw line. Jackson wanted to try the underhand toss that Bucky had demonstrated at The Good Earth, so he gripped each side of the ball, flexed his knees, and tossed the ball towards the net granny style. Swish.

"Well, I'll be danged," Jackson said. "Bucky was right. Let me try that again."

CHAPTER TWENTY-ONE

THE NEXT DAY BRENT RETURNED to basketball practice for the first time since the shooting. At the end of practice the whole team was shooting free throws on six different baskets. Brent was shooting bricks. He couldn't make anything. His mind was elsewhere.

"Come on, guys! You gotta concentrate!" Coach Howell yelled. "Try to swish every one. Try not to hit the rim at all."

Brent tried one underhand, just to see. He missed that too.

The whole team had been feeling defeated and aimless since the loss of T.J. Practices had no energy. Some boys felt guilty to even be on the floor without their team leader.

"Hey guys, bring it in." Howell shouted. "Fellas, bring it in. Let's go, c'mon!

The team gathered in the center of the floor.

"Guys, I know this has been tough," Coach Howell said. "This thing with T.J., it's hard on all of us. It's been a struggle. But somehow we gotta get our spirit back; we gotta get our energy and passion. You know when you came here two months ago to start the season, it was because you had a love for the game. And I know this has taken us away from that a little bit. And as you guys go through life, you're going to be faced with a lot of things, a lot of tough things that happen to you. And I think the true mark of a man is how you act when things are tough. I always think in terms of basketball, the starters who are starting and playing a lot, getting a lot of accolades, that's pretty easy. I always look at the tenth guy, or the eleventh guy, twelfth guy not playing much. How does he act? Is he a great part of the team? Is he supportive? And it's just one of those situations where we've got to all pick up and be together. And I know T.J. was important to us, and I know he scored a lot of our points."

"He scored almost all of our points, Coach," Jed said.

"Well, what are we gonna do about that!?" Coach was hollering now. "How 'bout you score five more, you score five more, you score five more," pointing fiercely, "and collectively we'll just play better defense! And we'll stay undefeated! Now you guys are making it real hard, 'cause I have got to find some way to get you out of this funk. So we're gonna go to the line. Let's go."

The guys moved out of the huddle slowly - too slowly for Coach.

"C'mon, let's go!" Coach Howell barked with feverish intensity.

The guys lined up at the baseline and sprinted away as coach blew his whistle. Gut busters, or suicides, meant they ran a quarter of the way down the court, touched the ground, headed back, and touched the starting line, turned around and ran to half court, touched the ground and came back, then three quarters and back, and finally full court and back. That was one. They were going to run a lot more than one. Coach Howell was just getting warmed up. He ran them, and ran them. Then he ran them some more, barking the whole time.

"C'mon, Ty! C'mon, Ty!"

"Good job, Brennan!"

"Way to work, Dylan!"

"Good job, Jed!"

Brent was falling behind everyone else. "C'mon, Brent, you're last! Let's go. Somebody's got to be last; it doesn't have to be you."

"Good job, Scott…"

Coach kept hollering, and the boys kept running. By the end of the tenth gut-buster, Brent was ready to collapse on the floor. As he crossed the baseline, he looked at Jed and said, "I'm done."

"At least it keeps our mind off the pain," Jed said.

Howell finally relented. "All right guys, we're done for the day. You can hit the showers."

"Brent, we've got to skip the showers; we've got to get to Earl's," Jed said, although he was dripping with sweat.

Brent sighed. He didn't want to go to Earl's, but he couldn't really tell that to Jed.

"I've got to at least change my clothes," Brent said, hoping to stall a little bit longer.

CHAPTER TWENTY-TWO

THERE WAS STILL DAYLIGHT LEFT when Brent and Jed walked out the gymnasium doors. Brent had his bike, and Jed, eager to get to Earl's, jogged alongside.

Brent was torn. Of course he wanted to help T.J., but at the same time, he wasn't sure he wanted Jed to actually discover anything. For the first time in his life, Brent couldn't tell whose side he was on. Part of him wanted to come clean, to tell Jed what had happened. But he couldn't. Had Sean bought Brent's silence with his money or his threats? As Brent pedaled and Jed jogged, Jed was talking but Brent wasn't listening. He was fixated on a piece of leaf that was stuck in the spokes of his wheel. It was going around and around and around. The leaf was stuck. So was he.

"How would we know how old T.J. is anyway?" Brent suddenly blurted out.

"What?" Jed had no idea where that question came from.

"Nothin'," Brent said. "Let's just get to Earl's."

Earl's Small Engines Unlimited was on the south side of town, not far from the high school. Across the street from Earl's

113

was a hill. From the top of the hill Sean and Mike could see the high school gym and the main street of town. It was a good spot to keep an eye on things, and Sean was interested in keeping an eye on Brent. They saw Brent and Jed leave the gym, and watched as Brent pedaled and Jed jogged alongside.

"I'm worried about your little brother," Sean said.

"He's not gonna talk," Mike answered.

"Maybe we should make sure of it," Sean said.

Mike was surprised to see the boys stop outside Earl's Small Engines. There was no reason for the boys to be stopping in for small engine repair.

Jed made it to Earl's door first. He burst right in and hollered, "Hey Earl, you in here?"

"Right here! Just give me a second," came a voice from the back room.

Brent lingered outside the store for a moment when his cell phone rang.

"Where are you?" Mike asked Brent.

Brent had no idea Mike was looking at him at the time, and he didn't want to tell him where he was or what he was doing. "At school," he lied.

Mike, who could clearly see that Brent wasn't at school, was glad that Sean hadn't heard that.

"Mike, I've been thinking," Brent said, "What if we just said that Frank was the one who fired the gun?"

"Why don't you tell Sean your idea," Mike said, and he handed the phone to Sean.

"Hello Brent," Sean said.

Brent was eager to try to bring some resolution to the situation. He was also worried that Jed's investigation could make things worse. He made a plea to pin the shooting on Frank.

"What if we just said it was Frank, we just say Frank shot the gun. I know that no one was supposed to get hurt, but what if we just went to the Sheriff and explained the situation, you know? And Frank's a jerk anyway. He would be the only one who would get in any trouble," Brent said.

"You do that, Brent," Sean said, with an edge to his voice that left no doubt about his implicit threat. "Find the Sheriff and give him a message. And then, I find your mommy, and I give her a message. Nobody tells nobody nothin'—that is how this works."

Brent's whole body shivered when he heard Sean mention his mom. He accidentally dropped the cell phone to the sidewalk. As he bent down to pick it up he caught a glimpse of a reflection in the shop window. The reflection was of Mike and Sean silhouetted on the top of the hill across the street from Earls. Brent realized they'd been watching him the whole time. He slowly stood up and tried to look calm, even though his heart was hammering. He wondered if either of them knew anything about the connection between Earl's Small Engines Unlimited and Frank's Camaro. He truly hoped not.

Jed had never been inside this store before, but it was obvious Earl was selling much more than small engine repair. Guns, for one thing, were a major part of Earl's inventory. There were racks of rifles behind the counter, and plenty of handguns for sale in the glass counter space just below the cash register. Throughout the store he saw a strange mix of fishing gear, hunting supplies, and musical instruments. An impressive collection of large animal heads were expertly stuffed and mounted on the wall above the door.

Jed was asking Earl about the Camaro.

"Did you find your records from the sale?" Jed asked.

"I tried to find the sales records, but I couldn't find anything. It's been six, maybe seven years," Earl said.

Brent wanted to get out of sight as soon as possible, so he walked into the store and joined Jed at the counter.

"Well, you must be Brent," Earl said.

"You must be Earl." Brent said, glancing back over his shoulder toward the hill across the street.

"You guys are having a real nice season. I come to every game. Such a shame about Lewis though. I sure hope he pulls through. You know, I figure that if they give some minutes to that kid on the freshman team – Osburn, I think is his name."

Jed tried to keep the conversation on point. He interrupted, "The car?"

"Oh yeah, the car. Well, you know I don't know if I'm gonna be any help to you guys."

"Can you tell us anything more about the car, anything at all?" Jed asked hopefully.

"Well it was old, but it was in pretty good shape. I take good care of all my vehicles. It had a cassette deck, black leather interior, I did the exterior in a real nice candy apple green…"

Brent hadn't really been listening, but was startled at the description. "What, what did you just say?"

"Huh?" Earl wasn't sure what part Brent was asking about.

"Nothin, um—you were describing the color," Brent said.

"Any way to find this car now?" Jed asked.

"Um, I don't think so. Unless, I might have my old insurance records; they might have the VIN, the vehicle…"

"Yeah, Yeah, Yeah," Jed interjected, "The vehicle identification number."

"I didn't think of that," Earl said.

"You find the VIN. I'll take it to the police and see if they can track the plate," Jed said.

"Wait a minute, I know—just give me another second," Earl said, and he headed into the back room.

Left alone together in the store, Brent was growing more uncomfortable with the situation by the second. He didn't want to find the car, and he didn't want his brother or Sean to find out he'd been looking for it.

"Jed, this is going nowhere; let's just go."

"He said to give him a second," Jed said. "We're going to find the car."

"Jed, we're not the cops."

Earl reappeared. He had a card in his hand with the information.

"Of course; it was with the insurance records. I was close. The guy's name was Frank Snelling; sold it six years ago for $4,000 bucks—pretty good deal."

Frank Snelling. Brent couldn't believe it. Jed had found Frank on his first try. Impossible.

"Do you have an address or anything for this guy, Frank?" Jed asked.

"I don't know if I should just be telling you guys this stuff," Earl said.

"Yeah, we understand…" Brent started to say.

"Earl, you give us that card, and we're going to find that car," Jed said with confidence.

Earl hesitated for a moment, then shook his head and held the card out in front of him. Jed snatched it immediately and gave Earl a big smile.

"Thanks, Earl," Jed said as he headed for the door, "I'm a customer for life!"

Earl watched Jed and Brent hustle out the door. "Great," he called out. "Maybe I'll get into bicycle repair!"

The card had an address: 10240 Indian Trails Road.

CHAPTER TWENTY-THREE

JED WAS PUMPED. MAYBE THIS was it; maybe this was the key that would lead them to the shooters. It wouldn't bring T.J. back, but it would at least serve justice.

"Let's go to the Sheriff," Jed said.

Brent knew that the last thing he could do was be seen heading into the Sheriff's office. He had to think of something to distract Jed, and he had to get out of there quickly.

"No, not yet. It's too soon." He started pedaling. "C'mon, I'll race you," Brent said.

"Where are you going?" Jed asked.

"Hardware store," Brent said as he pulled away.

"You going to see Butch?" Jed asked.

"C'mon—I'll meet you there."

Brent took off, and Jed tried to keep up on foot. There was no way; Brent was riding as fast as he could. The hardware store wasn't far; it was only a few blocks away off the downtown strip.

Brent was apparently taking the scenic route, because he cut down a back alley that led in the opposite direction.

Mike hopped on his motorcycle to follow after Brent and keep an eye on him. Brent was intentionally evasive. Mike came racing around the corner in the direction he thought Brent had gone. Brent peddled harder than he ever had. The Buell was loud, and Brent he could hear exactly where Mike was. Eventually he heard Mike driving the wrong way.

Jed made it to the hardware store with ease. Somehow he, on foot, had beaten Brent there. He stood outside by the front door and waited.

Brent finally came flying in on his bike from the opposite direction that Jed was looking. "You get lost or something?" asked Jed.

"No, I lost something, though." Brent looked behind him. "C'mon."

"What's going on?" Jed asked.

Brent rolled his bike into the Ace Hardware Store without answering Jed's question. He didn't want to leave his bike on the street where Mike might see it.

Their youth group leader, Butch Kooyer, was working behind the counter. Butch was Jed and Brent's favorite guy with a driver's license.

Butch smiled when he saw them. "Gentlemen. What's up?"

"You working late tonight?" asked Jed.

"No—we close in fifteen minutes."

Butch could see the eagerness in Jed's eyes.

"You must need a ride somewhere," he guessed out loud.

"We always need a ride somewhere," said Jed.

"Any news on T.J.?" Butch asked.

"No, nothing really new," Jed said, "But we've got a lead, and we need to check it out."

Butch was less than enthusiastic. "A lead? What are you now, detectives?"

"No, we're not," Brent said, "we're just..."

Jed cut in. "We need a ride out to—he pulled out the card Earl had given him, "10240 Indian Trails Road."

"That's a ways out there, I think," Butch said. "North side of the lake."

"Can you take us?" Jed was anxious.

Butch hesitated. "Um, it's supposed to snow tonight; my car's kind of crappy in the snow."

"Butch, your car's always crappy. And besides, Brent and I will push you out if you get stuck. C'mon, let's go."

"No, not just 'let's go.' I have responsibilities, fifteen minutes, and then... at least."

Butch pointed to the analog clock that hung above the front door. The time was 5:45. Jed moved quickly. He grabbed a step ladder, carried it over to the door, climbed up and grabbed the clock off the wall. He advanced the minute hand until it pointed straight up and showed Butch the clock that now read 6:00 on the nose with a big grin on his face. He hopped down and jumped back over in front of Butch at the counter.

"Now let's go."

CHAPTER TWENTY-FOUR

UTCH'S 1988 MUSTANG SOFT TOP may have been the least road worthy car in all of Charlevoix County. The heater didn't warm the car any more than the dome light did – which also didn't work. The AM radio worked though, and Butch was listening to a weather forecast. Jed sat in the passenger seat, Brent in the back. The plastic rear window was duct taped shut. The tape was the only part of the window that wasn't letting in cold air.

"Man, it's freezing in here! Could we turn on the heater?" Jed asked.

"It is on," Butch said.

"Oh," Jed said.

The radio announcer was predicting snow.

"… and it looks like plenty of snowfall tonight with temperatures dropping into the low teens. Gas up the snow blowers for sure…"

A light snow began to fall.

"Do you know where you're going?" asked Jed.

"Not really; punch up the address on this thing." Butch reached into the crowded glove box and pulled out a GPS. "Sorry, I lost the suction cup," he said.

Brent stared out the window and recognized the same roads he had traveled from the back of Mike's motorcycle. He couldn't think of a thing to do. If he objected too strenuously he would give himself away. If he didn't object he knew he was about to head back to the one place he absolutely could not be seen leading anybody.

Jed was playing with the GPS. "What language or accent would you like your directions in?" He asked.

"How about Spanish with a North Dakota accent," Butch said.

Jed pushed a couple of buttons and a computerized woman's voice said, *"Gire a al derecha en una milla."*

"I want to marry her," Butch said.

"I think she said to make a legal U-turn in five hundred miles," Jed said.

"She's a beautiful woman," Butch added.

The snow was coming down a bit more as they came to the narrow tree-lined street called Indian Trails Drive. Butch turned right, and Jed watched numbers on the mailboxes, searching for 10240. The driveways off Indian Trails Road were long two-trackers that wound back through the woods.

Jed saw the mailbox. "10240. This is it," he said.

"I'm not gonna be able to take the car down that," Butch said, looking down a long, dark, snow covered driveway.

Brent finally spoke. Maybe this was his out – the snow was too deep on the driveway! "Yeah, let's just forget it. We don't want to get stuck."

"No, pull over," Jed said. "We can just walk."

Of course, Brent thought.

CHAPTER TWENTY-FIVE

BUTCH PARKED THE CAR ALONG the side of the road. Jed and Brent climbed out the driver's door since the passenger door was permanently stuck shut.

A full moon was peeking through an opening in the clouds. Butch, Jed, and Brent set off down the driveway, the sound of snow crunching under their feet.

"This is fascinating work you've got us in here Jed," Butch said as he walked through the snow. "Fascinating."

"Hey, at least these woods are warmer than your car," Jed said.

"Ha, ha, ha," Butch replied. "Tell me again why we're out here walking down a stranger's driveway in the dark and cold."

"C'mon. I told you. We're looking for the car that I saw the night T.J. was shot," said Jed, who was a few steps ahead of the other two.

"And why aren't we doing this with the police?" Butch asked. "Your parents are not going to be very happy with me."

"Yeah, this is crazy." Brent objected. "It's one car; it's one random sale. There are millions of Chevy Camaros, and we don't even know anything. This is crazy."

Brent desperately wanted to turn around and get out of there before anybody saw him. But instead they kept walking. It was a long meandering driveway, and it hadn't been recently plowed. On top of that the snowfall was picking up. Finally around the last bend in the driveway they turned slightly to their right and saw before them a large classic shaped red barn. It was oversized, and on the end nearest them was an open window on the second story with a tall ladder leading up to it. Just beyond the barn was a small farmhouse that had a single light bulb dangling from its back porch. Brent, of course, recognized it all. To his relief, at least, it seemed to be deserted.

"Let's just go," Brent implored.

Just then, they each heard an approaching rumble echo through the forest. Loud thunder-like engines accompanied by distant crazy screams. The sounds were getting closer. All three guys stopped walking and listened.

"Okay guys, time to go," said Butch.

"Shhh!" Brent was panicked. He knew he could not be seen here; he absolutely could not be caught leading people right to the center of the Sean's meth compound. He knew the sounds of the engines were coming from Sean's collection of thugs. He assumed Mike would be with them.

The roar of the engines grew louder and closer – and then, suddenly, the sound was gone. For a moment everything just went quiet. Brent had momentary relief. Had they left? Turned around? It was short-lived relief.

Suddenly they heard the distinctive sound of a motor turning over and over, struggling to catch. It sounded like someone trying to jump-start a car without enough charge in the battery.

"Dude, what's going on?" asked Jed quietly.

"That's my car," Butch said.

"Did you leave the keys in?" asked Jed.

Butch reached into his pocket.

"No, I've got my keys right here."

The engine finally caught, and the motor revved and blared.

"I think that's my car! C'mon guys, we gotta go," Butch said.

Butch started running back up the long drive toward his car. Jed followed instantly, but Brent didn't move.

"Come on Brent, c'mon," Butch shouted.

"No, no, no—just go. I'm going to hang here," Brent said.

Butch stopped for a moment, "No Brent. You're coming with us."

"Mike can't see me out here," Brent said.

"Mike, your brother? What are you talking about?" Butch asked.

"It's probably nothing. Seriously, just go, and tell me what's up."

The noise from the road continued. Someone was clearly driving Butch's car, and now the rowdy voices coming from the road were rowdier than ever. It sounded like the Mustang was doing 360° doughnuts in the street.

"Fine, man. Butch—we've got to go," Jed said.

Brent took off running in the opposite direction.

"Brent! Brent!" Butch shouted after him.

As Brent ran, he shouted back, "And don't let anyone know I'm here!"

Brent headed for the old barn. The only thing he could think to do was hide. He made for the tall ladder leading up to the hayloft. While Brent ran away from the fray, Jed and Butch ran straight towards it.

CHAPTER TWENTY-SIX

BUTCH AND JED RAN AS fast as they could down the center of the driveway back toward Indian Trails Drive. As they drew close they ducked into the snowy woods and eased their way closer to the road. Hidden by the tall pines they saw eight or nine guys having a good ol' time at the expense of Butch's car. The Mustang was hopelessly stuck in a snow bank, although the guy behind the wheel was gunning the engine in reverse for all it was worth trying to muscle it out. He was going nowhere.

Another guy was jumping up and down on the hood of the car while the driver was honking and shouting something out the window. The rest of the guys were laughing at the spectacle. There was a mish-mash of snowmobiles and pick-up trucks scattered all over the road. The guy in the Mustang gave up trying to get the car un-stuck and jumped out of the car. Jed didn't know it at the time, but he was looking at Frank Snelling. Frank was stumbling around the car, obviously quite drunk, and in his right hand he carried a double barrel shotgun.

"Fine, fine, fine. You guys won't get me out of the ditch." Frank was shouting, "All right then. We've got to be professional. See what happens? Let this be a lesson to you; don't drink and drive."

Jed leaned toward Butch. "Butch, they've got guns!" Jed said.

"Yes, Jed, I can see that. Thank you," Butch replied.

Frank was holding court and prancing around the car, shotgun in hand. "We've got to put her down; we've got to put her down! We've got to put her out of her misery!"

The other guys were laughing, drinking, smacking the car, and giving Frank all the audience he wanted.

Frank pointed to the big guy who was dancing on the hood of the car, "Hey, hey, hey Bielman,"

Bielman jumped down.

"Say 'shave and a haircut,'" Frank said.

"Whaaat?" Bielman said.

"Say it, say 'shave and a haircut,'" Frank persisted.

"Just me?" Bielman answered.

"No, no—everybody. Everybody say 'shave and a haircut!'"

Frank cued them, and the whole gang sang it drunkenly together: "Shave and a haircut…"

"Two bits!" Frank shouted as he spun around and leveled the shotgun right at the front side of the car. He pulled the trigger.

BANG! Thwack!

The boom echoed long and far throughout the forest. The shotgun pellets shattered the front left headlight and sent pieces of glass and plastic flying everywhere.

"I got it! I got it!" Frank bellowed.

Butch winced as his radiator and left headlight were blown to bits.

"Butch, what do we do?" Jed asked.

Frank was so proud of his aim he shot the Mustang again.

Bang! Ping!

This time he hit the door.

"I'm going to call the police," Butch said, "But I need you to go back and stay with Brent. Okay? Stay with Brent until I get back."

"But what about your car?" Jed asked.

"Yeah, my car is pretty much out of commission, but my cell phone is in there. I'm going to wait until these guys leave and then get my phone. But you go back and stay with Brent till I come back."

"Are you sure about this?" Jed asked.

"No, I'm not sure about this. But we can't leave Brent out here alone. Go!"

"Okay," Jed said, and he took off running down the path. On the way, he heard the shotgun fire twice more.

Jed ran back down the driveway and scurried up the tall ladder leading to the hayloft. His boots clanged loudly against the metal rungs as he climbed. When he reached the top he was face-to-face with Brent, who was huddled in the shadows of the opening, looking out into the night.

"Dude, what's going on?" Jed asked.

"I'm just trying to lay low, you know," Brent said.

In the distance, they could still hear the gang laughing and hollering. Another shotgun blast rang out through the night.

"Why would you leave like that?" Jed asked. "They're shooting up Butch's car with a shotgun!"

"I heard it."

"Brent, this is serious. These could be the guys who shot T.J."

"I know it's serious," Brent said.

Jed climbed into the opening and crouched next to Brent.

CHAPTER TWENTY-SEVEN

Jed and Brent huddled in the opening of the second story hayloft and strained to hear what was going on back at the road.

"Where's Butch?" Brent asked.

"He's hiding in the woods hoping these guys will leave so he can get to his phone and call the police."

Brent sighed. That was the last thing he wanted to happen.

Just then they heard the snowmobiles start up. The entourage was heading down the long driveway, right toward the barn. The gang guys were as loud and obnoxious as ever, whooping and hollering the whole way.

Jed looked at Brent. "They're coming in here?"

"Shhh!" Brent said.

"You knew this was here."

"Just shut up," Brent said.

The sliding side door on the broad face of the barn was yanked open, and the lights came on. Jed and Brent were momentarily caught in the light, but they quickly pulled back farther onto the loft. Jed began slowly crawling, despite Brent's protests, closer to the edge of the loft so he could peer down and see what was happening below. Some of the snowmobiles were driving straight into the barn, some were parking outside.

Frank made a grand entrance, laughing and bragging non-stop. He was still carrying the 12 gauge. He was only three steps inside the barn when Sean stepped in front of him. Sean was furious.

"Frank, you stupid moron!"

"Shut up, Sean, or I might—bang!—blast you, too!" Frank was very drunk.

"Frank, the whole point of being out here in the middle of nowhere is to *not* attract attention. You might as well have just put a sign out front!" He snatched the gun from Frank's hands.

:)

Butch remained hidden in the woods until he was sure all the guys were completely gone. His feet felt like they were frozen solid. Finally he limped out of his hiding place and ran to his car. The Mustang was steaming and hissing like Old Faithful. The radiator was obviously destroyed. There were silver pockmarks all along the passenger door. The grill was shattered.

He reached in through the open window and pulled his cell phone out from the glove box. He flipped it open, but the phone stayed dark.

"Ahh, dead," Butch said to no one in particular.

He couldn't call, but he needed to find a way to get the boys out of there. He headed down the road and stuck his thumb out at the first pair of headlights he saw. They drove right past without stopping. He kept walking.

In silence Jed crawled closer and closer to the edge of the loft. Brent was freaking out, afraid someone was going to see him. He shook his head as forcefully as he could. Jed kept going anyway and slowly peeked out over the edge of the loft. Below him he saw the same group of guys he'd seen out at the road, plus a couple more. He saw Mike. He saw a small fire stove in one corner of the barn, an assortment of motorcycles and snowmobiles here and there, and two long tables strung together upon which a lab had been set up. He suspected they were cooking up drugs. There was a very strong and distinctive smell – he thought it smelled like a hospital. In the back corner of the barn, Jed spotted a nylon drop cloth that looked like it was covering a vehicle. The shape of that nylon looked like it could well be covering the car he was looking for, a vintage 60's Camaro.

CHAPTER TWENTY-EIGHT

BUTCH KEPT WALKING DOWN INDIAN Trails Road hoping to thumb a ride. After a while a pick-up truck approached from the east. Butch stepped part way out onto the road and waved his arms. The truck slowed and stopped, and Butch jumped in.

Just minutes after Butch rode away in the pick-up truck, Deputy Davis of the Charlevoix County Sheriff's Department came around the bend of Indian Trails Road and saw the still-smoldering wreck of Butch's Mustang, half buried in the ditch.

He called it in. "Dispatch, this is 3-11 Zebra. I've got a white Ford Mustang on Indian Trail Road, License: N68 984. It looks pretty beat up. I'm going to get out and investigate."

Davis pulled his flashlight and slowly got out of his car. He approached the vehicle with caution, flashlight in his left hand and his right hand resting on the holster of his unclipped pistol. He looked in and around the car. There was nobody in the car, but fresh footprints were everywhere in the snowy street. Spent 12-gauge shotgun shells left an unmistakable clue to what had happened. Davis went back to his car to call in again.

"Dispatch, this is 3-11 Zebra. I've got shotgun shell casings and holes in the car. I'm going to proceed to 10-240 Indian Trail Road and investigate suspicion there."

Big Mack was out in the woods taking a pee when the Sheriff's car stopped by the Mustang. Mack realized there might be trouble. He sprinted back to the barn, flew in the doors, and shouted at the top of his lungs.

"We got cops, people! We're going dark!"

Everyone inside moved quickly. The truck was brought in the barn, the fire was doused, the sliding doors were shut and locked from the inside. The whole gang hustled down the wooden steps into basement. Brent was terrified. He was trying to figure out whether there was any way that Sean might be able to connect the arrival of the Sheriff with him. He was sure that Butch had called the cops.

Snow was falling hard now, and even the recent tracks were covered. The barn was completely dark and quiet by the time the patrol car arrived. Deputy Davis approached the barn slowly, quietly, and with his headlights off. He stopped the car, opened his door and gingerly stepped out. With his flashlight he painted long arcs along the base of the barn. His right hand stayed on the pistol in his holster.

Jed and Brent were watching from the hayloft.

"Maybe we should jump down there and tell them we're here," Jed whispered.

Brent grabbed him with all his might. "Don't move!"

Jed wasn't sure why they shouldn't move, but for some reason he honored Brent's request and kept quiet. Several times the beam from the flashlight passed just over their heads. Brent kept his arm tight over Jed to ensure he didn't change his mind.

Deputy Davis was more than a little suspicious about the barn, but he didn't have a warrant to enter the premises, and he didn't have any backup. He knew he could be walking into a hornet's nest if he pushed the issue prematurely. He went back to his car and drove off, fully expecting to return shortly with a few fellow officers.

CHAPTER TWENTY-NINE

JED AND BRENT WERE SHIVERING as they watched the patrol car drive away. It was bitter cold, and they'd been lying still for a long time.

"I have really got to pee," Jed whispered.

On the main floor of the barn Bielman opened the sliding door, clicked on the lights, and called out loudly, "He's gone."

Sean and the rest of the gang emerged from the basement. Jed slid quietly to the edge of the loft again and watched the scene below. As the last of the gang emerged on the barn floor, Jed saw Sean grab the guy who had been wielding the shotgun by the collar.

"That was stupid, Frank. The cops were here because of you."

Jed perked up when he heard the name. That could be Frank Snelling, the same Frank who bought the Camaro from Earl.

"I'm sorry," Frank murmured. "I know—I'm drunk. I under..."

Frank never finished his sentence. Sean's right boot flew up and kicked him square in the groin. As Frank doubled forward in pain, Sean hit him with a vicious uppercut that caught him square in the nose and flipped him backward. Blood poured everywhere.

"That's nothin', Frank," Sean said as he stood over him. "That is nothin'."

Frank answered weakly, "It's nothin'... it's nothing..."

Sean looked at Frank and slowly pulled the Glock out from his coat. He twisted the gun sideways and pointed the barrel right at Frank's head.

Frank began begging for his life, "No, no, Sean, no! I'm sorry, I'm sorry! I didn't, I mean, I won't do anything, I promise."

"This is not nothing," Sean said calmly.

"No, Sean, you don't have to shoot. You don't have to..."

Sean pulled the trigger and the gun exploded with a thunderous boom and a flash that lit up the whole barn. Frank instantly dropped to the floor. Jed thought he was dead. Frank wasn't dead – he was still whimpering.

Sean laughed a little bit. "If you ever do something stupid like that again, Frank Snelling," he said calmly, "I won't miss."

The guys in the gang stood around nervously. Sean was starting to scare them a little bit now.

"We have to leave," Sean barked. "They'll be back. Leave the bikes; leave everything. Move!"

Guys moved. Snowmobiles and trucks were started. It didn't take long to empty the place out. Mike lingered behind, and Sean pulled him in close and whispered something into his ear. Mike nodded. Sean walked out of the barn, and Big Mack turned out the lights and closed the sliding barn door behind him.

Jed and Brent watched as the pickup trucks and snowmobiles disappeared in the distance. They waited silently for a long time after that. Finally Jed could wait no longer.

"Let's move," he said, still whispering. "I've got to see what's under that tarp, but I gotta do something first."

Jed stood and moved toward the window at the top of the ladder.

Brent whispered back. "Good idea."

They stood at the edge of the opening and peed out into the dark night. The streams fell forty feet to the ground.

CHAPTER THIRTY

JED CRAWLED SLOWLY AND SILENTLY toward and along the edge of the barn loft, feeling for the top rung of the ladder that would take him to the ground floor. The only light drifting into the barn was moonlight from the open hayloft window. Even with that Jed had difficulty seeing where he was going. But he had to know what was under that tarp; he had to know if he had found the Camaro.

The ladder, once he found it, was just a bunch of short boards nailed to a vertical support beam. Slowly, he rolled over onto his stomach and inched his toes down until they found the ladder's top rung. His legs and body were stiff, but he gingerly put his weight on the first board and began to descend. The boards were old, and Jed hoped they would hold his weight. Thirteen tentative steps later, he made it to the barn floor. The dim gleam of moonlight coming through the second floor opening did little to illuminate the ground level under the hayloft.

Jed assumed he was alone in the barn, but he continued to move as quietly and slowly as he could. He inched across the floor with his gloved hands out in front of him, feeling his way toward the far back corner where he had seen the nylon tarp. That tarp

could be cloaking the key that would unlock the crime. For a moment, he thought of T.J. lying helplessly in a hospital bed.

Jed's outstretched hand bumped against the chrome handlebars of one of the Harleys, and he felt his way along the bike to the wooden posts of another support beam. Jed inched his way across the barn, past the rusted metal hinges of the stable doors, past the still warm heat of the fire stove, past the meth tables, and finally to the car buried in the far corner.

Jed ran his glove along the front right rear fender of the car as he moved slowly to his right and bent down low. He felt the stiff rubber treads of a tire. Now he was perfectly oriented, and he knew what he had to do. He reached up till his hand discovered the door handle. For some reason the nylon tarp had already been pulled back over the passenger door. Odd. He remembered the car being fully covered. He carefully pulled on the chrome latch.

As the door opened, the interior light came on, along with a ringing bell sound. Jed saw exactly what he expected to find—the black leather interior of a 1968 Chevy Camaro. What he didn't expect to find was a person sleeping in the back seat. A person with a pistol in his hand.

"What the heck…" groaned Mike as he woke suddenly, the unexpected light assaulting his eyes.

Jed slammed the door and ran.

"Let's go!" he shouted up to Brent, quietly but urgently. He backtracked as quickly as he could through the dark barn floor toward the ladder steps. Brent was still waiting at the top of the loft.

"What? What?" Brent gasped.

Just then the car door opened and Mike fell out of the car onto the ground. He'd been awakened from a deep sleep and was a bit delirious. The gun clattered to the ground as Mike yelled out, "Who's there?" Who the heck is there?"

Jed didn't have time to go back up the ladder the way he'd come down. His next thought was to just head for the barn's slider doors. He got there quickly but discovered they were locked. The lock was nothing but a simple bolt dropped through a swinging hitch but Jed's gloves were just bulky enough that he couldn't get a quick grip on the bolt. He had no time to fuss with it, so instead he stumbled down the stairway to hide.

Mike was quickly able to recover his senses. He picked up the gun and grabbed a small Mag flashlight off a shelf. He was angry now. He turned on the flashlight and swept the beam of the flashlight around the floor level of the barn. The light swept over the meth lab, the wood stove, the motorcycles. The light fell over the stairwell, and Mike started to move in that direction. Brent saw what was about to happen, so he ran across the loft upstairs, making a distracting noise to draw Mike's attention away from the stairwell where Jed was hiding.

"Frank, is that you? What's going on?!" Mike headed for the ladder and began to ascend.

As Mike was nearing the top rung of the ladder, Jed made his move. He emerged from the dark stairwell, removed his glove, pulled the bolt out of the latch, and opened the sliding door. As he sprinted out the door, he heard the roar of two high performance snowmobiles racing down the long driveway, coming straight towards the barn.

"That's gotta be Butch!" Jed shouted, hoping Brent would hear him.

Brent was swiftly climbing down the long metal ladder from the hayloft. He recognized those snowmobiles too. This was their escape, he just had to get there.

149

The two yellow Ski-Doo snowmobiles flew down the long driveway toward the barn at breakneck speed. When they reached the barn they laid down a pair of perfect180-degree power slides right in front of Jed and Brent. The drivers were wearing matching lime green snowmobile suits with bright yellow helmets and visors. They were each carrying an extra helmet, and they quickly tossed the helmets to the boys.

"Let's go! He's got a gun!" Jed screamed. He and Brent each jumped on the back of a snow machine and held on tight.

The yellow Ski-Doos had incredible acceleration. They burst away from the barn with such speed that both Jed and Brent nearly flew off the back. They hadn't gone far when a super-sized black Arctic Cat came screaming out of the barn in furious pursuit.

The snow was coming down hard now. Brent felt like he had just gone into Star Wars hyper drive. The white snow, illuminated by the Ski-Doo headlights, was flying past his visor like a warp speed galactic blur.

Although Jed only caught a brief glance of the guy in the backseat of the Camaro, he was sure it was Brent's older brother Mike. He didn't think Mike had gotten a good look at him, however. Brent knew exactly who it was in that car, and on the snowmobile chasing them. It was Mike, and Mike absolutely couldn't know that Brent had been anywhere near the barn.

CHAPTER THIRTY-ONE

THE YELLOW SKI-DOOS WERE BUILT and tuned for racing. They consumed big chunks of snow with rapid bites as they practically flew down the long driveway. They moved like they were trying to catch up to the beams from their own headlights.

Jackson had Jed on the back of his ride, and behind them Butch was driving with Brent holding on tight. They blew past the entrance to the long driveway and cut hard to the right, past the crippled Mustang, and down the snow covered pavement of Indian Trails Road.

Mike was only a few seconds behind them, and he had no passenger, which made him even faster. He cut the corner at the end of the driveway, hit the incline of the embankment, and flew twenty feet before the treads of the Arctic Cat track re-engaged with the fresh snow.

Brent looked behind him and saw the headlights of the black Cat gaining on them. He urged Butch to go faster. Jackson, driving the lead snowmobile, swerved hard to his left and cut through the vacant fields of a dormant farm. Butch and Brent stayed right on his tail. They raced around an old barn, across a short field, through a wide gate, and accelerated alongside a never

harvested row of field corn. The corn stalks flew past them like fence posts behind an Indy car. But despite all their maneuvers they could not shake Mike. If anything he was closer than ever.

Jed peered back at the two snowmobiles following him and realized that they needed a new strategy.

"Split up! Split Up! He yelled as loud as he could. Yelling through the facemask of a snowmobile helmet is tough, and Jed's attempts to communicate over the roar of racing engines operating at full throttle was nearly futile. He waved his arms in a wide pattern, and Butch got the idea. The two Ski-Doos raced directly toward a dead end and at the last second Jackson cut to the right and Butch veered to the left. The move caused Mike to pause for just a moment as he decided which way to turn. He chose left, and stayed on the tail of Butch and Brent.

Butch drove his machine as hard as it could be driven. He leaned hard into each turn and did everything he could to evade his pursuer. He was headed for the highest point in the county, the top of Mt. McSauba. He knew the mountain trails well. He climbed and climbed, but the Arctic Cat stayed right on his tail.

Brent was hanging on for dear life. He turned around and saw the Arctic Cat now about a half a football field behind. When he looked ahead, it looked like they were about drive off the end of a cliff. They were at the top of a steep decline known as "Suicide Hill." At the base of the hill was an outdoor skating rink, and at this hour of the night there were still skaters on the ice under a string of twinkling Christmas lights.

Butch pointed the Ski-Doo straight down the hill and gunned it. By the bottom of the hill, they were going insanely fast. At the base of the hill Butch cut hard to the right, pulled the snowmobile up onto one ski, and flew by the rink and the startled skaters. But the Arctic Cat stayed with them. Mike had too much at stake not to find out who had blown their cover.

Just beyond the ice rink Butch turned left onto an unplowed county road. The long straight road cut through thick trees on either side. There was no way to pull off this road. This was an advantage for the Arctic Cat, and there was nothing for Butch to do but pull the throttle all the way to the hand grip, put his head down, and let her fly.

Butch suddenly recognized a bigger problem; he was about to crash into a truck! There was a stop sign ahead, and the road came to "T". A big semi truck was driving from left to right on the "T" road. They were on a collision course. Butch didn't really have the option of slowing down.

The truck driver saw the headlights of the Ski-Doo coming from the street to his right. He could tell they weren't slowing down, but there was nothing he could do. A truck of that size wasn't about to come to a quick stop on snowy roads, so he laid on his air horn.

Brent saw the truck. He didn't know if they had enough speed to beat it. It was going to be close. The stop sign grew closer, the truck kept coming, the Ski-Doo held its speed. Brent closed his eyes. The honking harmony of the truck's twin horns blasted into Brent's left ear but thankfully the truck didn't. Like a yellow flash the Ski-Doo passed in front of the semi, barely, and crashed through the underbrush on the far side of the "T". Butch and Brent ducked their heads just under the low hanging branches, and emerged unscathed into a wide-open cornfield on the other side.

Mike, however, had no chance to beat the semi. If he tried to gun his Arctic Cat, he would have plowed straight into the side of the big truck. At the last second, with the semi dead in his path, Mike cranked the handlebars hard to the left. The Arctic Cat went tumbling sideways into the snow bank, treads in the air and driver flying. The impact cracked the hood, bent the skis, and stalled the engine.

As the semi-truck rolled away and the yellow Ski-Doo raced out of sight, Mike threw his helmet into the snow and shook his fist in disgust.

CHAPTER THIRTY-TWO

ONCE FREED FROM THEIR PURSUER, Butch decelerated to a more normal speed and headed for home. He pulled up in front of his winterized Airstream trailer. Jackson and Jed rode in from the north and arrived at the trailer at almost the same time.

"Woo'ee!" Jackson shouted, as he pulled his helmet off. He shook his hair in the moonlight and launched into his NASCAR broadcasting voice. "They're taken' them turns at dangerously high speeds, Jim Bob. I'm not sure we've seen driving like this on the circuit since the glory days of ol' number three…"

Brent was impressed. "Not bad, Jackson," he said. "Where did you learn to drive like that?"

"Many talents, boys. They don't call me Mr. Everything for nothing."

"They don't call you that," Brent said.

Butch cut in. "Are you guys done, because we need to talk."

"We've got to call the Sheriff, 'cause I think we found the car," Jed said.

"I already called the Sheriff. Are you sure it's the same car?" Butch asked.

"Oh, man," Brent sighed and turned away from the others. Now the Sheriff was going to get involved.

Jed continued talking to Butch, "I think so. There was an old Camaro under a tarp, and it was kind of dark, but I'm pretty sure it was green."

Brent was pacing. "Mike was out there tonight," he said. "But..." Brent struggled to find the words.

"But what?" Jed asked.

"But, look, Mike will kill me if he thinks I'm the one who called the Sheriff."

"Brent, that was your brother in the back of that car, and he had a gun. If he's involved in shooting T.J..."

"But he wasn't," Brent said.

"Well, how do we know?" Jed answered forcefully. "We know he's involved with a gang, we know he's hanging out in a barn with them, and we know they're hiding a Camaro under a tarp!"

"But we don't even know if that's the car," Brent said.

"Well, so what? Let the cops figure that out. And we do know they shot up Butch's Mustang."

Jackson piped in. "Shooting? Butch, you never mentioned any shooting."

"Jed," Brent said.

"What?"

"Look, when the Sheriff gets here, tell him about the car, and tell him about the gunshots, but don't tell him about Mike. Promise me, Jed."

"No." Jed answered.

"You guys better figure it out; he's here," Jackson said as the swirl of red and blue lights began to wash over their faces.

The patrol car pulled up next to Butch's trailer, and Sheriff Clayton McDonald stepped out.

"Evening, boys," he said, as he walked up to them.

Jed stepped right up. "Sheriff, I've got an idea who shot T.J., and we probably should have called you first, but we had no idea what we were going to find, so I thought if we checked it out, so we could, just in case, you know, be certain, and also I thought you probably wouldn't take us seriously. I'm sorry we didn't come to you first, but.... "

"Slow down, son," Sheriff McDonald said. "Just tell me what happened."

"Well," Jed took a breath, "I saw the car, and I'm good with cars so I thought maybe we could find it. So we went out tonight, and I think we found the car. It's in this barn," he said as he pulled the card from Earl out of his pocket, "at 10240 Indian Trails. We went out to find it, but they had guns out there, and they shot up Butch's car and then they chased us out."

"They, who is this they?" the Sheriff asked.

"I don't know who they are, but they were in the barn, and they all left."

Brent noticed that Jed had not mentioned Mike by name.

"All right," the Sheriff said as he turned to leave.

"Where are you going?" Jackson asked.

"Well, to the barn to find that car."

"Can we come? Can I show you?" Jed asked.

The Sheriff shook his head and opened the door to his patrol car, "I'm sorry, son. I think I can take care of this myself."

As the Sheriff drove away, Butch opened the door to his trailer. "Come on guys, let's go inside."

But Jed was putting his helmet back on.

"What are you doing?" Butch asked.

"We're going back to the barn," Jed said as he hopped back on the Ski-Doo.

"Whoa, what?," Butch protested.

"Shooting, you said there was shooting," Jackson said.

Jed just pulled the starter and fired up the snowmobile. They were going back to the barn.

CHAPTER THIRTY-THREE

JED HAD TO KNOW IF he'd actually found the right car. He wanted to be there when the Sheriff found it in the barn. He was worried maybe the gang would move it, maybe it wouldn't be there by the time the police arrived. If the car was missing, he wanted to be able to show the Sheriff where it had been sitting. To Jed this car was the key to putting away whoever had was responsible for shooting his friend. But as they turned back down the long driveway off Indian Trails, Jed instantly knew something had gone drastically wrong. Above the trees there was a bright glow. Something was on fire.

Brent, Jed, Jackson and Butch stepped off their snowmobiles, took off their helmets, and stared in disbelief. A massive inferno lit up the surrounding forest, and they stood before the biggest fire any of them had ever seen. The entire barn was in flames. Flames burst from the rafters, climbing high into the night sky. The long ladder Brent and Jed had climbed earlier in the night was now glowing red. The intensity of the heat coming from the flames was frightening.

"There goes our evidence," Jed finally said.

If the Camaro had been in that barn, it was completely incinerated now. They were back to square one.

:]

It was well past midnight when Jed finally made it home. He was tired, confused, and frustrated. He had come so close. On top of everything Brent was acting totally strange, and Jed didn't know what to make of it. He kicked off his shoes, grabbed his laptop computer, and flopped down on his bed.

He checked his messages. There was another one from T.J.

His exhaustion instantly disappeared. Suddenly he was upright and wide-eyed, staring at the screen. He clicked on the message window.

God will not take over until I cross this threshold. I don't know how to do this, really. T.J.

Jed read the message three times, but he couldn't understand it. What threshold? Was T.J. talking about life and death? Jed pulled out his cell phone and hit a speed dial button.

"Brent, are you up?"

"No, I'm asleep," Brent answered, lying in the darkness of his bedroom.

"Yeah, I know it's late. I got another one, another message from T.J."

"Huh?" Brent lifted up and turned the lamp on next to his bed.

"I'll read it to you. He says, "God will not take over until I cross this threshold. I don't know how to do this, really.""

"You think this means he's dead?" Brent asked.

"No."

"You think he's trying to tell us something?"

"I don't know. I don't know what to think," Jed said. "It's all just really, really weird."

"Yeah," Brent didn't offer anything more.

Finally, Jed decided to confront him. "Brent, what's goin' on?"

"I don't get it either Jed."

"No, Brent, with you. You know more than this. You know something."

Brent squirmed in his bed.

"I gotta keep my mouth shut, Jed."

"Brent, it's me," Jed waited.

Brent said nothing. For some reason he suddenly remembered the day he, Jed, Jackson and T.J. had caught that big fish off the pier. On that day Brent remembered making a promise to himself that he would never hide anything from his best buddies. They were all so innocent, so happy-go-lucky. That was before his dad left, before Sean came to town, before he and Mike somehow got mixed up in this whole incredible mess. Now he was lying to Jed – again. The one guy in the whole world he could really trust. He couldn't admit to his best friend that this whole thing was his fault, so he said nothing.

Jed decided not to push the issue. He figured Brent would talk when he was ready.

"Anyway, goodnight," Jed hung up.

He fell back into his bed and read the message one more time.

"God will not take over until I cross this threshold."

This time Jed didn't assume that T.J. was out of the coma. But somehow Jed was still getting these strange messages. What in the world was going on?

Brent couldn't sleep either. He stared out the window as voices, images, memories, and fears ran continuously through his mind. He wanted to tell his mom; he wanted to tell someone the truth; he wanted to run away and hide. All of those options seemed impossible. He also didn't know if Mike had figured out who he had been chasing. He felt like a prisoner of his own mind.

When his alarm went off at 6:30 a.m., Brent didn't feel like getting out of bed. He was bone tired, and he was deathly afraid of confronting Mike. He hadn't heard Mike come in, and he was hoping he still wasn't home.

Brent snuck out his bedroom door and walked as quietly as he could down the hall to the bathroom. He was almost to the door when he heard the toilet flush. Dang! There was nowhere to hide, so he just leaned up against the wall and dropped his eyes to the floor.

"Well, look what the cat dragged in," Mike said as he walked out of the bathroom. Mike just walked right past Brent and went back to his room.

Brent was relieved. Mike didn't know! He hadn't recognized Jed in the barn, and he didn't know who he'd been chasing. As Mike just walked away down the hall, for the first time Brent knew something in the equation that Mike didn't.

CHAPTER THIRTY-FOUR

After school on Tuesday, the Rayder's gymnasium was filled with the familiar squeak of rubber-soled shoes on hardwood courts, and the reverberating boom of dribbling basketballs.

The team was scrimmaging – white shirts against black. Jed and Brent were on the black team, the team made up of the starting five. Coach Howell blew the whistle and raised his hand in a fist.

"Let's go, Jed! Run the offense!" he yelled.

Jed had the ball, but his mind was far from focused on basketball. There was a wide hole in the heart of the team, a hole where T.J. was supposed to be. Jed had played sports with T.J. from the first week that the Lewis family had moved to town. At first, it was soccer, or "bunch-ball," as T.J.'s dad had called it. When they were in mini-mite soccer, everyone on the team pretty much just ran toward the ball and kicked it as hard as they could. Sometimes it went in the right direction, but usually it went right into the other guy's shins.

And there was hockey. Jed had learned to skate as soon as he learned to walk, and wintertime pond hockey behind their house

was always fun and brutal. There were Little League Baseball teams, Pop Warner Football teams, school track teams - Jed couldn't remember being on a team apart from T.J. at his side. Playing on a team without T.J. was like trying to tie your shoes with one hand.

Now Jed was dribbling too much, and coach wasn't happy.

"You gotta move! You gotta move! Too much dribbling, Jed! Too much dribbling! C'mon, Bracken, pass the ball, get your head up! That's too much dribbling."

Jed dribbled down the baseline and under the basket. He finally looked up and fired a pass to Brent who was standing at the 3-point line. Brent caught the pass and heaved an off-balance shot that missed badly. He turned and jogged down the floor. The white team grabbed the rebound and broke down the court quickly.

"Get back, get back! Come on, Brent! You've gotta get back!" Howell implored.

Brent's man got behind him, caught a pass, and made an easy lay-up. Brent was way too late to stop it.

Disgusted, coach blew the whistle again. "Hold up fellas, everybody bring it in right here!"

The players gathered right at center court of the old gymnasium. Light was streaming in through the semi-opaque windows at the top of the arched dome. Howell's voice echoed in the empty cavern.

"Brent! What's goin' on? What kinda shot was that? That's your team's possession. That's a shot for your team. And then you made the second mistake—you don't run back!"

Coach Howell was getting louder.

"And you know what? It's contagious. You see the rest of your teammates? What'd they do? They didn't hustle back either."

Brent looked down at the floor.

Coach changed his tone. He softened.

"You know, T.J.'s not here. And we're all struggling with that. Me, you guys, our community. And last night, you know, I'm lying in bed thinking, *What can we do to maybe send a message that we're in this together and we're gonna make it?* And I thought, maybe if we all got a nice collared shirt and a tie, and we wear that on game day, maybe the community would see us, see that we're bonded together."

"Coach, I don't have a tie," Brent said.

"You don't have a tie? Can you get one from your fathe..fa... um... You know what? Anybody else not have a tie?" Coach asked.

Five or six hands went up.

"This is what we'll do. I'll raid the closet tonight; I have enough ties for everybody. We'll meet at 7 for breakfast. I'll make sure everybody's dressed right, properly, how we want to be, and we'll take a few minutes to teach you how to tie a tie. Teach you how to dress like men. We'll have a little learning experience together, have a little fun with that, and we'll plan on that. I'll see you tomorrow. All right, guys. That's it."

CHAPTER THIRTY-FIVE

AFTER PRACTICE THE RAYDERS WERE showering and changing in their maroon and white cinderblock locker room. Jed sat on the bench in front of his locker. One of his teammates, a junior named Lyndon, sat down next to him and began unlacing his shoes.

"You have a tie?" Lyndon asked Jed.

"Nope. But I can borrow one of my dad's."

"I know how to tie a tie," said Hayden.

Hayden was the Rayders' center. He was a big guy. Brent coiled up a long towel and tossed it to Hayden.

"Well, let's see it then Mr. Grown-up Man," Brent said.

"Okay, it's very simple." Hayden said, and he wrapped the towel around Brent's neck and began to tie a knot.

"You take the wide end like this, loop the narrow end underneath, and tighten until the head turns purple."

Everyone laughed except Brent, who yanked the towel off his neck, spun it into a rat's tail, and snapped hard on Hayden's backside.

Jed stood up. "I see we're learning to act like men already."

:]

Jed and Brent were the last two to leave the locker room. When they came out the door, Jackson was standing in the hall waiting for them.

"Hey guys, sorry I missed practice," Jackson said.

"Jackson, you don't have to watch practice," Brent said.

"Coach chewed us out today," Jed said, "and we have a new dress code."

"I'm not wearin' a tie," Jackson said.

"You're wearin' a tie," Jed and Brent said in complete unison.

"All right, I'm wearin' a tie," Jackson conceded. "I went to the hospital today."

"Did you see him?" Jed asked.

"Not really."

The daylight was gone in the late winter afternoon, and the air was bitter cold. It didn't take long for wet hair to freeze on a day like that. Jed's hair was short and it dried quickly. Brent's curly hair was frozen by the third step he took outside.

Just outside the gym, Reverend Lewis' Trail Blazer pulled in.

T.J.'s sister Jordyn climbed out of the car. "Can you pick me up around eight?" she asked her dad.

"Of course," Rev. Lewis answered.

Jed caught her eye. They didn't even say anything. He just gave her a hug. They shared a deep grief, and neither one knew what to say.

"Thanks, Jed," Jordyn let a tear drift down her cheek.

Reverend Lewis rolled down the passenger window, "Want a lift, guys? It's cold out here."

Jackson leaned in, "I went to the hospital today. Can you tell us anything?"

Reverend Lewis didn't answer right away. "Let's go get something hot to drink," he said. He had something important he wanted to discuss with them.

The guys piled in, and he drove them all down to The Good Earth.

CHAPTER THIRTY-SIX

THE WAITRESS AT THE GOOD Earth placed four steaming mugs down on the table. This night the boys didn't sit on their usual barstools; they sat at a table by the woodstove. Brent stared at his hands, afraid of what might be said, and afraid of what he couldn't say. Reverend Lewis stood five feet from the table, cell phone to his ear, pained expression on his face. Finally, he hung up, sat down and joined the boys.

"You okay, Reverend?" he asked.

"You guys never knew my wife, Pam, did you?" Reverend Lewis said. "Oh, I really miss her. She loved God, loved people, loved animals."

"T.J. told me about her," Jed said.

Rev. Lewis was acting sort of distracted. He changed topics.

"You guys knew T.J.'s heart," the Reverend said. "T.J. knew God. T.J. - he trusted God with his life."

"Of course he did," Jackson said. "His dad's a minister; what choice did he have?"

Jed socked Jackson in the arm.

"No, no, I mean it. T.J. was the kind of guy who would give his life to save someone else's," Reverend Lewis said.

"T.J. *is* that kind of guy. T.J. *would* do that. And he's gonna make it through this. Don't give up hope Reverend," Jed said.

"Hope? I have hope. I have eternal hope in Heaven," Reverend said. "But I have to make a decision."

"What kind of decision?" Jackson asked.

"There's this girl in Minnesota; she was in a car accident, and T.J.'s a match for her. I have to decide about an organ donation."

Brent stared at the floor, Jackson stared into his mocha, and Jed looked straight into the eyes of Reverend Lewis.

"No, don't do that. We just can't give up hope now," Jed said.

"Jed," Reverend Lewis placed his giant hand on top of Jed's on the table, "there's been no brain activity. I've been sittin' there for days, staring at that EEG machine, just hopin' and prayin', hopin' and prayin'."

"Don't do it! Don't do it—not yet, anyway," Jed said. "Say no. I've got to tell you something, and I don't know if you'll believe me."

Jed hesitated, but everyone else kept quiet.

"It seems like T.J.'s been, somehow, contacting me." He paused again. "I'm getting messages from him on my computer."

"What?" Jackson said. "That's just mocha you're drinking, right?"

"There's been two of them now," Jed continued. "They're from T.J. I don't have them with me, but I could show you. I think he's trying to tell me, tell us, something."

Reverend Lewis reached across the table. "Jed, the Bible talks about a still, small voice. The small voice is real, but it is the Spirit of God, not the voice of a dead person. We are not to try and talk with the dead."

"But T.J.'s not dead, is he? And these messages on my computer—I'm not hearing that. I'm just reading. You could come over. I could show you."

Reverend Lewis stood up. "I've got to go," he said.

"Reverend, when do you have to make the decision?" Jed asked.

"Soon. Very soon."

Reverend Lewis walked out the door. Jed stared straight ahead.

"He's given up," Jackson said.

"Not me," Jed replied.

Brent never said a word the whole time.

CHAPTER THIRTY-SEVEN

On Friday each of the Rayder basketball players wore button down shirts and ties. A couple of them had nice tight knots, but most of the guys looked like a big wad of cloth had gotten stuck between their collars. By game time the players were happy to put on their uniforms and lose the formal wear. They had postponed two games and were taking the court for the first time without their captain. Nothing felt right.

The Rayders did their normal pre-game stretching and warm-up routines. Coach Howell did his best to give a game plan review and pep talk. Marcos DeAndies was now starting at shooting guard and Jed would move over to play the point. Marcos had always wanted to be a starter, but not like this. He seemed almost embarrassed when they introduced him before the game.

The energy in the stands was nothing like it had been at previous games. The fans were subdued; even Jackson was sitting down. He clapped his hands and shouted, "C'mon, boys! Here we go!" But it was at about half his normal volume. He was, at least, wearing a tie over the top of his lucky sweatshirt.

Petoskey was the opponent, Charlevoix's longtime rival. Petoskey was the next town up the Lake Michigan coastline, only seventeen miles to the north. The Petoskey players were well aware of the situation with T.J. Lewis. T.J. had been beating them at various sports for years, but these were healthy rivalries. Athletes often had the most respect for their toughest opponents. T.J. had been their nemesis, but he was never their enemy.

The Petoskey players displayed proper respect, but they had come to play a game. They were not about to go easy on a team that was 10 and 0. Petoskey had only lost two games, both early in the season, and they were climbing through the standings, now tied with Elk Rapids at 8 and 2.

Hayden lined up for the opening tip. He almost always out-jumped the other team's center. The Rayders rarely even practiced defending off the opening tip. The referee tossed the ball in the air at center court and the game was underway—at least for one team. The toss went up a moment before Hayden was ready to jump, and he was caught flatfooted. As soon as the ball went up, a Petoskey forward broke straight for the basket.

"Brent, watch your back. Brent!" Coach Howell was yelling.

The Petoskey center didn't tap the ball backward like a usual jump ball; he punched a volleyball spike straight down the court to the forward who was there all alone. He got a basket uncontested. The score was 2-0 before the Rayders even moved.

"Come on, Brent! Get your head in the game!" Howell shouted.

But Brent didn't. He retrieved the ball from under the basket and casually tossed it inbounds toward Jed along the baseline. He didn't see the Petoskey player who broke right in front of Jed and laid in another easy lay-up. It was now 4-0, and the game wasn't even ten seconds old.

And the game went downhill from there.

The Rayders played defense like it was somebody else's job. On offense they jacked up desperate shots from well beyond the three-point line. None went in. Petoskey couldn't miss; it was like they were shooting at a rim the size of a hula-hoop.

Charlevoix's shooters had no rhythm, no jump, and no touch. They fell further behind with each passing minute. Coach Howell jumped to his feet and called a timeout. Jed sat down in the middle of the huddle, but Brent kept himself out at the edge. Basketball was not on his mind.

"Listen up," said Coach, "You're too tentative. Jed, take some chances; you are allowed to shoot the ball. Brent, beat your man off the dribble; he can't stay with you. Hayden, Marcos—get some rebounds. They're in a simple 2-1-2 zone, so pound the seams guys. You know how to do this."

Jed's parents were in the stands.

"This doesn't matter like it used to, does it?" said Jed's dad. His wife put her hand on his knee.

"No. It just doesn't," she answered.

By halftime, Charlevoix was down by seventeen points. It was by far their biggest deficit of the season. The team sat in the locker room waiting for the coach to come in, sure they were about to get a tongue-lashing. Everyone's head was down.

Coach Howell finally entered.

"Wow. You know I came walking in here, and I was trying to think of something positive to say to you guys after that performance out there. And I'll be honest with you. I can't think of one thing that went well out there. And I don't understand. We've been through so many things. We've run. We've talked.

We're trying to get through this. Does anybody in here have any other ideas?"

There was a long, silent pause. The guys weren't used to criticizing their own performance; that was the coach's job. Nobody knew what to say.

Hayden finally spoke up. "Well, we're standing around on defense, not helping out, not switching."

"Anybody else?" Howell asked.

Brent's mind was racing. He knew he'd played terribly. But worse than that, he blamed himself for the whole ordeal. If he hadn't gone out to that barn, if he hadn't taken that money, if he hadn't told Sean about the skating rink, T.J. would be in the locker room right now. Brent wished he were the one in the coma. At this moment he would gladly trade places with T.J. Finally, he blurted it out.

"It's me," he said softly. "I'm so terrible. I am ruining this team." Brent wasn't really thinking about basketball. "I'm sorry guys… I'm so sorry." He was biting his lip and fighting with all his might not to lose control in front of the team.

He lost the fight. He couldn't hold it in any longer. He started crying—sobbing—and he couldn't make himself stop. He slid off of the bench and fell onto the floor, with his head between his knees. Jed had never seen Brent cry before; in fact, he couldn't ever remember anybody crying in the locker room.

Jed got on his knees and put his arms around his friend. Brent couldn't stop the tears.

Jed spoke quietly into Brent's ear, "You haven't ruined anything. Just play; just get out there and play. We're with you."

A moment later the other players followed Jed's lead. Coach Howell and all ten of the other guys got down on the floor and extended their arms toward or around Brent.

The referee stepped into the locker room to give the second half notice. He stopped – he'd seen a lot of halftime speeches, but he had never seen an entire team on their knees in the middle of the locker room before. It looked like they were having a prayer meeting. "Um, two minutes, Coach," he said sheepishly.

Brent's breathing began to relax.

"Frontier Boys, we don't give up on each other," Jed whispered to Brent.

"Thanks, Jed," Brent said.

It was time to play.

CHAPTER THIRTY-EIGHT

As BRENT ENTERED THE GYMNASIUM for the start of the second half, he felt lighter. He had made a decision. He wasn't going to live a lie anymore, and he didn't even care what happened to him. If he could protect his mom, he was willing to accept whatever came to him. But first, he was going to play basketball as if it was the last game he would ever play.

Petoskey took the ball at mid-court to start the second half. Brent walked slowly onto the hardwood floor with his head down as he lined up next to his man. His back was to the player in-bounding the ball. Brent took a chance. Just as the Petoskey guard tossed the pass in to start the second half, Brent timing it perfectly, spun around and stole the pass. He drove uncontested to the hoop and laid the ball in. The stands began to come alive again.

From then on, Brent stuck to his man like glue. The Rayders applied the full court press, and the energy from that opening steal seemed to electrify the whole team. The Petoskey center who was trying to inbound the ball couldn't find anybody open, and the five-second count was almost up. He called timeout.

The fans began to cheer a bit louder as the players ran over to the coach. Howell kneeled down on the floor and looked straight

into their eyes. "Men," he said, "Win or lose, nobody comes in here and outworks you. Nobody."

:]

Reverend Lewis wasn't at the game that night. It was the first Charlevoix basketball home game he had missed in years. Tonight he had something else on his mind. He drove his truck down to the shoreline of Lake Michigan and stepped out into the evening air. An icy wind blew across the steel grey lake. The cold air hit his skin like a swarm of tiny needles. He jammed his hands into his pockets and walked along the frigid boardwalk. He needed to make a decision.

:]

Jed felt the fire coming back into his legs. He was determined to do what his coach had asked—to work as hard as he could the rest of the game and let the results fall where they may. He put his hands into the center of the team circle and shouted, "One, two, three, team!"

Petoskey managed to get the ball in-bounds this time, but that was about all they got. Charlevoix's double team closed so fast on the man with the ball that he didn't even have time to turn around. He tried to make a return pass to the man who had inbounded the ball, which was exactly what Jed expected he would do. Jed intercepted the pass and drove it right to the basket for another easy lay-up. They were now down by only thirteen.

Petoskey suddenly realized that the second half was not going to be the cakewalk the first half had been. The Rayders seemed to be moving at double speed.

"Defense is about one thing," Coach Howell always said, "Desire. If you're willing to work, you can always play good defense. You can stand back and watch the other team move and pass, or you can move your feet and disrupt what they want to do. It's all about desire."

Petoskey finally got the ball across the timeline, but they couldn't penetrate. They didn't come close to getting off a good shot. As the shot clock wound down to zero, Petoskey's guard launched an off-balance twenty-five footer. It clanged off the side of the backboard. Hayden got the rebound and spun around and passed the ball to Jed at mid-court. Brent was flying down the right side. Jed saw him out of the corner of his eye and made the same sort of volleyball spike pass that the Petoskey center had used at the start of the game. His tap pass was right on target, and Brent went up and dunked it. In a flash the Rayders were down by only eleven.

:]

Reverend Lewis refused to yield to the cold. He walked along the icy boardwalk and cried out to God, desperately seeking a word, a touch. He believed that T.J. would want to save a life. T.J. would want this, he thought. Yet actually making the call to the hospital was proving to be the hardest thing he'd ever done. He pulled his cell phone out of his pocket. He put it back again. Once he made this decision, once he made this call, there was no turning back. Once he gave permission to harvest his son's organs, any shred of hope he held onto would be gone.

:]

Under the mercury vapor lights of the old Charlevoix gymnasium, the basketball game continued. Something different, however, had taken over the spirit of the Charlevoix team. If defense was desire, as Coach said, then offense is momentum. As the game began to swing Charlevoix's way, success begat more

success. Shots began to fall; the circumference of the rim seemed to grow for the Rayders.

The best way to play basketball, or just about any sport for that matter, is to play loose and relaxed. "Don't think; just play," Coach Howell would say. Coach talked about getting in *the zone,* that indefinable space where one's body just seems to know how to get the job done without interference from the brain.

"The funny thing about *the zone,*" Howell said, "is that once you think about it, or even become aware of it, it goes away. *The zone* only happens when you get so lost in the game itself that you just play. Your brain hardly even seems to get involved. Your body just takes over, goes into auto-pilot, and does what it knows how to do."

For the second half, Jed and Brent were in *the zone.* They weren't thinking; they were just playing.

Pump fake.

Get the defender in the air.

Take the contact.

Bank in the shot.

Three point play.

Fast break.

Fill the lanes—full speed.

Pull up at the free throw line.

Make the defender commit.

Look right.

Pass left.

Uncontested lay-up.

Cheat off your man.

Anticipate the pass.

Steal the ball.

Another fast break.

The point gap began to close and the crowd grew louder and more excited. The game and the moment became the only thing on Brent's mind. The pursuit of a come-from-behind victory was enough to momentarily help everyone forget the tragedy, enough to make everyone share a few moments of hope.

Reverend Lewis looked up at the moon as it peeked through the dark clouds. He was looking for God and he didn't know where else to put his eyes. T.J.'s neurologist had said that there was no activity whatsoever in T.J.'s brain. The coma was as deep as ever, and the machines that regulated T.J.'s breathing and heart rate were still the only things keeping him alive. Those machines could not be kept on forever.

Reverend Lewis pulled out his cell phone one final time and began to dial T.J.'s doctor. With every press of a digit, he felt like he was executing his own son.

CHAPTER THIRTY-NINE

THE DEFICIT WAS ONLY THREE points now. Charlevoix was loose, focused, and confident. Petoskey, as often happens when a team tries to protect a lead, had become uptight and self-conscious.

Petoskey called a timeout. Their coach was yelling at them in the huddle, exhorting them to step up, to play with poise.

"Poise, boys," he liked to say.

But the more they tried to think about playing with poise, the more their brains messed up the natural skills they had for the game.

Brent was playing like a maniac. He had always been fast, and now he was using that speed every time he touched the ball. Fake left, drive right. Stutter step, lean back, blow by his man. Brent had fourteen points in the second half alone.

Jed's man was now going over to double-up on Brent to try to stop his penetration. As soon as Brent recognized the double team, he quickly passed the ball to a wide-open Jed. Jed shot it as soon as it touched his hands. The next thing it touched was net. One-point game.

:]

Reverend Lewis hung up the phone. He had done it. He had approved donor options on T.J.'s liver, spleen, and heart—a heart that a girl in Minnesota needed to survive. The doctors from Minneapolis had been waiting on stand-by alert. The moment the word came in, they sent a pilot and a doctor on a small charter plane to fly to Michigan for the organ harvest. After that, it would be over.

Reverend Lewis sat down on the cement wall and repeated the words Jesus himself had said the night He went to the cross, "Not my will, but Thy will, Lord. Not my will, but Thy will. Not my will…"

:]

There were forty-eight seconds to go, and Petoskey had the ball. The crowd was excited now, and Jackson had joined the cheerleaders down on the floor. He faced the crowd and led a cheer, making it up as he went.

"We are the Rayders!" Jackson yelled.

"We are the Rayders!" The cheerleaders and crowd repeated.

"The mighty, mighty, Rayders!"

"The mighty, mighty, Rayders!"

"Boogity Boo!"

"Boogity Boo!"

"Wackity wack!"

"Wackity wack!"

Following Jackson's lead, everyone got down very low, brought it up, and threw their hands over their heads as they yelled, "Biggity, biggity, biggity, biggity, biggity, biggity, wheeeeeeeeee!"

It was about the stupidest fight song cheer of all time, but Jackson led it with such passion that everyone went with it. He was in his zone again too, waving his pom pon in one hand, his Rayders pennant in the other. With a black marker he had written the number 23, T.J.'s number, on both sides of his pennant.

The game clock was at twenty-seven seconds and counting down. Petoskey had a one-point lead and the ball, but they would have to shoot with at least three seconds on the clock, that is if they could get a shot off at all. Jed, Brent, Marcos, Hayden, and Lyndon were on the floor, and they were swarming around their opponents like bumblebees. What the Rayders really wanted was a steal or a jump ball—the possession arrow pointed their way.

Petoskey was determined not to go down easily. With just six seconds on the clock, their big center got the ball in the paint. He pivoted and went up as if he was about to shoot. Two Rayder defenders jumped up with their arms straight over their heads to block the shot, but the Petoskey player didn't jump at all. It was just a head fake, and as soon as the defenders were off their feet, he took one dribble, spun around them, and laid in a nice left-handed reverse lay-up. With four seconds to go, the scoreboard read: Home: 51, Visitor: 54.

CHAPTER FORTY

AT SKYWAY AIRFIELD IN ST. Paul, Minnesota, a medical technician and a pilot took off in a six-seat Cessna. Valerie Lee, a sixteen-year-old patient, lay still in her hospital bed, unaware that the gift of life she needed would soon be on its way. Her mother and father held hands and prayed to God for the gift they needed. Valerie didn't have much time.

:)

The radio announcer for the Rayder basketball team was summing up the contest.

"Well, folks, if you've just tuned in, Charlevoix, with four seconds left, is down by three. A lackluster first half to say the least..."

In the huddle, Coach Howell was focused on the positive. "Fellas, fellas, that was a great effort to get back where we are."

Coach was back on one knee in the middle of all his players. He had his white board out, and he was diagramming their path to victory.

"All right. Now we've got four seconds. We have to have a three. It can't be a two; we're down three. And here's what we're gonna do. Jed you're gonna make this, and we'll win the game in overtime. So you're gonna be all on your own. You're gonna hit and blast. We're gonna feed you there. You gotta take one hard dribble toward Hayden and make a sharp pass to Hayden. Brent you're coming in; we're gonna set the flair screen. You're coming off the flair screen. We're gonna go over the top, and you're gonna be wide open. Make sure that you forwards drift down to the corners, and it should be all there—wide open for ya. Finish it up, and let's go to overtime, fellas! Great comeback! All the way back! Now, let's go! Team on three, one, two, three. TEAM!"

The play-by-play announcer spoke into the microphone. "You know it's hard not to talk about T.J. Lewis, the absence thereof, as Charlevoix tries to win this ball game with three seconds left."

The second announcer added, "Well, our hearts just go out to his family and friends." He had no idea how true his words really were.

The referee blew the whistle and handed the ball to Brent. Brent passed the ball in to Jed. Jed passed it to Hayden at the top of the key as Brent came in and set a pick on Jed's man. Jed broke to the right and Hayden lobbed the ball over the top to him. He caught it and in one motion rose for an open jump shot right at the three-point line. The play worked just as designed. As the ball arched toward the hoop, the game buzzer went off.

The ball had perfect backspin and a nice high trajectory. Jackson, like everyone else in the building, saw the seams of the ball rotating backward as it floated toward the hoop. You could almost read the word "Wilson" as the ball descended toward the rim.

The ball hit the rim on the back side, just a fraction of an inch too far. It was halfway down, but it rattled out. A collective groan went out from the Rayders crowd as cheers erupted from the Petoskey bench and cheerleaders. The Rayders had suffered their first defeat.

Jed was stunned. The shot had felt perfect. He thought he'd made it. Lara and Libby, a couple of Jordyn's friends, were the first to reach him on the floor.

"I'm so sorry," Lara said.

"You can't win them all, right?" Libby added.

Jackson walked up. "Of course you can win 'em all. Jed, you got mauled on that shot."

Jed just took a deep breath and lined up to shake the hands of the other team.

:]

From six thousand feet over Wisconsin, a Cessna pilot called ahead to confirm the weather in Northern Michigan. With everything clear, he anticipated being on the ground in Charlevoix in about an hour and forty minutes.

:]

Reverend Lewis kept his eyes looking toward the west, and he kept repeating his prayer, "Not my will, but Thy will be done. Not my will, Lord, but Thy will."

CHAPTER FORTY-ONE

Brent took longer than usual to shower and change after the game. By the time he and Jed emerged from the locker room door, the hallway was nearly empty. Jackson, however, was still waiting.

"Man, Jed," Jackson said, "I can't believe those blind referees couldn't see you getting hacked on the last shot. Are you even okay?"

"Nobody touched me, Jack," Jed said calmly.

"Yeah, well, that's not the point," Jackson said. "It was definitely the refs. Gambling scandal probably."

Brent looked at Jackson and smiled. It was the first time Jed had seen him smile all week. "Carlson," he said, "you ever get depressed about anything?"

Jackson put his hand on Brent's shoulder and stood up straight. "I am the eternal optimist. I believe every putt is in the hole, every stock is going up, and every girl in the school is secretly crazy about me." The fact that Jackson didn't play golf, didn't own stock, and had yet to go on his first date with a girl was irrelevant.

Brent turned to Jed. "Thanks for what you said at halftime. Now I've got something I need to do. Frontier Boys—no matter what, right?"

"Brent, I meant what I said," said Jed. "That's what family is, right?"

Brent turned to walk out the door, "Not always."

Brent walked out the door with the purposeful stride of a man who had someplace to go. As soon as he left, Jed's mom and dad came around the corner.

:]

Office hours were long over at the Charlevoix County Sheriff's Office. Sheriff McDonald was just leaving the building and heading for his car when he saw Brent Fencett riding up the sidewalk on his bike.

"Sheriff!" Brent called out. He came to a stop. "I have a confession to make."

The Sheriff looked into Brent's face and saw a young man who was serious and convicted about something.

"Let's go inside," he said.

Sheriff McDonald led Brent to a small interrogation room near the back of the office. Deputy Davis was still at his desk, and when Brent and the Sheriff closed the door, Davis put on a pair of headphones to monitor the conversation.

Brent wasted no time. He told the Sheriff the whole story, including the part he had played in the shooting and the cover up. Brent figured he would not be walking out the front door that night, but would instead be locked in one of the small cells in the back.

When he finished his story, the Sheriff put his pen down and looked Brent square in the eye.

"Brent," the Sheriff began, "I don't think you caused this. I think you tried to stop it, but you should have come to me sooner—threat or no threat."

Brent just nodded.

"Now you want to make this right."

"Yes." Brent said.

"I've got an idea. Hang on a moment."

Sheriff McDonald exited the room. Brent just stared at the table the whole time. Then the Sheriff returned carrying two tiny silver cylinders.

"Know what these are?" he asked.

"Nope," Brent answered.

"They're trackers. Here's the deal. We need to catch up with Sean. We know a lot about him, but we don't know where he is. Now, your brother might know. If one of these little do-dads just happened to get on Mike's bike and one on his truck, sooner or later, it could lead us to Sean."

"So, why don't you guys just put the trackers on Mike's truck?" Brent asked.

"Brent, where does your brother keep his bike and truck?"

"In the garage."

"Exactly, and we can't go in there," the Sheriff explained. "No judge will give me a warrant with the evidence I've got. But you can go in there. Now, I know you're a minor, and I can't officially ask you to do anything here, but you know—I'm just saying."

Brent stared at the two trackers sitting right in front of him on the table.

"Now, if you'll excuse me, I think I need a fresh cup of coffee," Sheriff said. "Would you like anything?"

The Sheriff stood up and stepped to the door.

"Wait," Brent said. He looked up, "Can you protect my mom?"

"You have my word," the Sheriff answered.

Sheriff McDonald left Brent alone in the room. Deputy Davis approached him outside the interrogation office.

"What do you think you're doing? You can't ask a kid to place homing devices!"

"I didn't ask him," the Sheriff answered.

"Well you might as well have," Davis said. "Besides, we don't even need them. We've got Mike under surveillance 24/7."

"I know," the Sheriff said.

"So again, I ask you, what in the world are you doing?"

"Ken, you ever screw up? Hmm? Ever do something so lousy you thought you could never live it down? Guilt like that can eat away at your soul. That boy in there needs to feel like he's made a good choice for a change. That's where I come in. Helping him feel like he did something right."

While they were continuing to talk, Brent snatched the two trackers and left out the side door. Sheriff McDonald saw him out of the corner of his eye and smiled.

CHAPTER FORTY-TWO

JED WALKED HOME FROM THE game alone that night. He had plenty of time to think about the game, about the shot he missed, about their first loss. He felt empty. It wasn't that he'd missed the last shot — it was that he had to be the one to take it at all. That should have been T.J.'s shot. He came in through the garage and shuffled his way toward the kitchen. His mom was just hanging up the phone.

"That was Reverend Lewis," she said. "He said he's made a decision."

Jed dropped his gym bag on the floor and sat down on a barstool next to his mom.

"A decision?" He instantly knew what the decision would be. He looked into her eyes. He felt a giant lump forming in the back of his throat. He couldn't help himself. His friend was gone.

"They're going to take his organs, aren't they?" Jed asked.

"Soon," Judy Bracken nodded.

Jed sighed. His eyes began to cloud. He knew the consequences. Suddenly all their efforts at finding the shooters, all the energy

and optimism he'd felt from the e-mails, all of it seemed like a colossal waste. He didn't know what to say.

"Mom—could you pray?" he asked.

Judy Bracken took her son's head in her hands and pulled him in. Her baby boy was now fifteen years old. She wished she could protect him from the pain, she wished she could absorb some of it into herself – but she couldn't. She kissed the top of his head, and breathed out a deep breath.

"Jesus," she whispered. "Comfort my son. Because—I can't."

Jed could no longer hide his tears.

"Heal his friend, Jesus."

They stayed in that embrace for a long time. Jed hadn't clung like that to his mother since he'd been an infant.

Finally he said, "I have to go."

Jed wanted to go to the hospital for a last goodbye, but first he went upstairs to his room and checked his messages. As soon as he opened the computer screen, he saw another one—another message from T.J. This time he didn't call anyone; he didn't run outside. He just read the message.

> *Good things come—sometimes we have to wait. It's getting better. Pray again.*

Jed bowed his head, "I won't stop praying for you, T.J."

About that same time, Brent arrived home from his visit to the Sheriff. For the first time in two weeks, he felt free of the never-ending guilt that had shrouded him. He had confessed, and he was willing to face whatever consequences came his way. He also was ready to take action against his own brother. He just needed an opportunity. He walked in through the front door of his house and found both his mom and brother in the kitchen.

"Hello dear," said Brent's mom. "Sorry I couldn't make it to your game. How did you do?"

"We lost."

"Oh, I'm so sorry. But you've still won more than you've lost, right?"

"Right."

Mike moved toward his brother. "Oh, you lost, huh," Mike said mockingly.

He grabbed Brent's face with his right hand and squeezed his cheeks. "Look at you—you look like a tiny fish."

Brent was tired of Mike's abuse. He'd taken it for years. Brent shoved Mike away with more force than Mike expected. Mike lost his balance and slammed back into the refrigerator.

"Boys, be nice to each other," Lois said. "Let me make you something special for dinner."

"Not me. I'm leaving," Mike said. Brent was a bit stronger than he'd anticipated. The kid had grown. Mike wasn't ready to have his physical superiority challenged.

"Where are you going, Michael?" asked Lois.

"Book club. It's *Grapes of Wrath* this evening," Mike said in an overtly sarcastic tone.

As usual, Brent's mom didn't notice, she remained oblivious to everything that was going on around her.

"Well at least have some quesadillas and pop before you leave." She said in a sweet voice as she pulled out four cheese quesadillas from the oven. That was her idea of something special for dinner. A couple tortillas with shredded cheese and Coke.

Brent moved through the small kitchen past Mike. He looked at the cookie sheet and the quesadillas. "Save me some," he said. "I've gotta go to the bathroom."

As soon as Brent left the kitchen Mike grabbed all four of the quesadillas and bit into the whole group of them at once. It was Mike's lame retaliation for the shove.

Brent didn't go to the bathroom; he quietly stepped into the garage. If Mike was about to leave then Brent had to act quickly. He pulled one of the trackers out of his pocket and held it in his teeth. The garage floor was messy and wet and Brent didn't want to get any slush on his knees, so he dropped down in push-up position and reached underneath the rear wheel well of Mike's truck. The magnetic tracker sensed the nearby metal and jumped right into place.

Brent popped up and moved toward the motorcycle, but before he could do anything he heard Mike open the door to the garage.

"I don't have time for dessert, and I'm not doing dishes. Deal with it." Mike yelled at his mom.

With only a split second to act Brent simply grabbed Mike's helmet and dropped it into the freezer. At least that would prevent Mike from taking off on his motorcycle, Brent figured. And since he hadn't placed the tracker on the bike yet, that seemed like a good solution. Brent stood over the open freezer and pretended to look down into it, as if searching for something to eat.

"You better find something in there," Mike said as he came into the garage. "I finished all the delicious quesadillas. I'm sorry."

"Thanks," said Brent.

Mike threw his leg over his bike as the garage door opened. He always left his helmet hanging on the left side of the handlebars. He reached for it instinctively. It wasn't there. "Where's my helmet?" he looked at Brent.

"Are you kidding me?" Brent said. He shrugged his shoulders as if to say, you think I would ever touch your helmet?

"Fine then, I'll just drive." Mike didn't seem to suspect anything. He simply climbed off the bike and got into his truck.

Across the street in an unmarked police car, two surveillance officers were watching the house. The one in the passenger's seat grabbed his walkie, "He's moving."

"Don't lose him," said the voice of Sheriff McDonald on the other end of the radio.

CHAPTER FORTY-THREE

Jed and Jackson slowly walked together through the intensive care unit at the Charlevoix Hospital and turned into T.J.'s room. T.J. lay motionless on the bed as his friends paused at the doorway. There were so many wires and tubes connected to T.J. he looked like he'd fallen into an oversized spider web. The silver plastic respirator tube was stuck all the way down T.J.'s esophagus, and it sounded like a gurgling dishwasher that never turned off. Next to his bed were three monitors, each displaying different patterns of green light.

A nurse named Sandy was adjusting a bag of fluid that was connected to an intravenous tube, dripping something into T.J.'s right arm.

"You serving him dinner?" Jackson asked.

"You could say that," the young nurse said.

"What are those monitors for?"

She pointed to the one on the left, "This one's an ECG, an Electrocardiogram. It measures heartbeat." The green lines on the screen were spiking up and down in regular intervals.

"And this one monitors the airflow through his lungs controlled by the respirator." The monitor displayed a different rhythm, but nonetheless a regular one.

The third monitor was completely still.

"And this one?" Jed asked, pointing to the third.

"That's the EEG—Electroencephalogram. Measures brain activity."

"And it's not moving at all," Jed commented.

"No, it hasn't," said Sandy. "We've tried to induce brain activity, but so far, nothing."

The pause in the room was heavy. Both boys felt like her words had formed into weight on their shoulders. It felt terribly strange to be so close to him and yet feel like he was so far away.

Sandy continued, "We've got machines to make the heart beat and the lungs breathe, but nothing to turn the brain back on."

Brent appeared in the doorway. "Hey," he said, without emotion. "How's he doin'?"

"Not so well," Jed responded. "They're making him breathe, making his heart beat, and feeding him goop in a tube."

"Nurse says they got nothin' to fix a broken brain," Jackson said.

The lights from the lighthouse raked across the icy shoreline and frozen parking lot as Sean once again assembled his makeshift gang for the evening's marching orders. Mike rolled up in his black pickup truck and as soon as he hopped out of the door, Big Mack tossed a roll of black duct tape at him. He didn't see it coming. The tape hit his arm and fell to the ground.

"Tape your plate," said Big Mack. He was bent down at the back of another old pick-up truck, covering its license plate.

Mike put the tape over the numbers on his license plate, and walked to the center of the group. Sean was waiting.

"You're late," Sean said.

"I'm here," Mike growled.

The gang closed in around Sean, ready for instruction.

"All right. The address is 37 Pine," he told them. "It's an operations center for the Mexican gang that's been controlling the supply, and tonight we're going to send them a little message."

Sean held up two Molotov Cocktails, tossed one to Mike, and the other to Big Mack.

"Now I've only got two of these," Sean said, "So aim good."

Mike gave his cocktail to Frank.

"You toss it," Mike said.

Frank was surprised and delighted with the assignment.

"Fine," Sean approved. "In that case, Mike you lead; just keep an eye out for cops."

"Where are you gonna be?" Mike asked Sean with a hint of suspicion in his voice.

"I'll be along." Sean answered with a glare.

The trucks and motorcycles pulled out belching visible exhaust in the cold air of the evening. Mike's truck led the convoy, with Frank and Nikko riding in the back. It was cold, but they weren't going far. Frank was giddy with excitement.

Sean watched them drive away, but he made no move to follow them. As far as he was concerned, this would be the last time he'd have to lay eyes on any of them.

Sean's driver pulled the Audi Q7 up and rolled down the driver's window.

"I didn't know there was a Mexican gang in town," the driver said.

"There isn't," Sean laughed.

Sean had made his decision. This group had failed the audition. He was done with this ragtag group of guys. Mike had been wrong, he hadn't delivered a few good men; he'd delivered idiots. They had already drawn too much attention, had burned down their own operation, and they hadn't yet produced or sold a single thing. Sean was leaving town, and he was setting Mike and his buddies up to take the fall.

"So, are we done here?" the driver asked.

"Almost," Sean said. "Call it in, call 911."

The driver dialed and calmly reported suspicious activity at 37 Pine.

Sean got in the Audi, and they drove away in the opposite direction. Sean had one more stop to make, then he would disappear.

Nurse Sandy grabbed a clipboard and walked out of the hospital room. The Frontier Boys were together again - the four of them - alone for the very last time.

As boys, the four of them had been alone together so many times. There was the custom two-story tree fort they'd built when they were in the third grade, the private screening of the *Transformers* at 2 a.m. they had been able to arrange at the local theater, numerous getaway weekends at Jed's grandparents' cabin, trips to Tigers games in Detroit, countless nights lying on the beach looking up at the stars, long evenings playing roller hockey in the driveway, van rides all over Northern Michigan on the way to baseball, football, or basketball games, New Year's parties watching bowl games, Halloween nights collecting pillowcases of candy, winter retreats at Spring Hill camp, and summer hiking trips.

These four boys had spent the bulk of their childhood together, but one thing they had never done was hang out in a hospital. Brent moved toward the bed. He knelt down beside the T.J. With tears in his eyes, he whispered into his ear.

"I'm sorry, T.J. I'm so sorry. I never meant for this to happen. I'm so sorry. Can you forgive me?"

Jed and Jackson stared, bewildered. After a long, deep breath, Brent turned to them.

"Guys, there's something I have to tell you."

CHAPTER FORTY-FOUR

INSIDE THE HOUSE AT 37 Pine the Sanchez family was spending a quiet and typical evening at home. They were about to play the card game Euchre. Maria Sanchez, fifteen, was watching TV in the living room when she was summoned to join the rest of the family back in the dining area for the card game. She pulled herself up from the couch and stretched.

Mike turned his truck onto Pine Avenue. The rest of the gang followed him. Two pick-ups and four loud motorcycles came tearing down the street like a gang of outlaws riding into town. They were an intimidating sight. Mike came to a stop in front of 37 Pine as Frank lit the Molotov cocktail.

"Watch this, Nikko," Frank said as he jumped out of the bed of the pick up.

Frank, flaming bottle in hand, ran up to the porch and shouted, "Hey! Free drinks everybody!"

Maria paused. She heard voices right outside her window. She turned.

Frank threw the bottle.

Fire came crashing through middle of the picture window. The Molotov cocktail hit wood floor and exploded. Maria screamed and was knocked to the floor. Shattered glass sliced into her skin. Her father jumped up from the table, grabbed her, and rushed her out the back door. He had no idea what was going on, but one thing he did know: his living room was in flames.

Mike didn't wait around. Frank jumped back into the truck and Mike began to pull away, feeling brave and victorious in battle.

He didn't pull far. Instantly his path was blocked by two patrol cars that seemed to appear from out of nowhere. Sirens blared. Mike slammed on his brakes and threw the truck into reverse. But before he could back up two more squad cars pulled right behind him and blocked his only route of retreat. Police were everywhere with guns drawn.

Sheriff McDonald was already out of his car and on the bullhorn. "Get off your bikes and come out of your cars slowly. Come out with your hands up, and don't even think of making this worse for yourselves than it already is."

Mike hadn't expected this. There were flashing lights everywhere, and the sounds of more sirens were getting closer.

Two ambulances were racing toward the burning house at 37 Pine Street. Four volunteer firefighters had heard the dispatch. Fire trucks from the closest station had already pulled out of their garages. It would take less than three minutes for all of them to converge on the 37 Pine. It sounded like the U.S. Army was closing in.

Mike realized he had been set up. He was in deep trouble. Before he knew it, the Sheriff was cuffing his hands together behind his back and reading him his rights.

"Mike Fencett," the Sheriff said, "You have the right to remain silent. Anything you say may be used against you in the court of law. I'm hereby charging you with aggravated assault, reckless use of firearms, and attempted murder. And if T.J. Lewis doesn't make it through the night you can add Murder One."

Mike looked at the officer with desperation in his eyes. He raged against the restraints, but he could barely move. He was firmly under control of the Sheriff, who steered him forcefully toward the back door of the squad car.

"Sean! Sean!" he yelled.

Sean was nowhere to be found.

"Sean can't help you now, tough guy," Sheriff McDonald said. "Get in the car." He shoved Mike into the back seat of the patrol car and slammed the door.

Within ten minutes, all the sirens were silent. Water poured out of fire hoses onto the silent licking flames that danced through the windows of the Sanchez's front porch. Paramedics began treating Maria as she lay on a stretcher next to the ambulance. And nine tough guys who had set out less than thirty minutes earlier to stir up a little trouble were now wearing handcuffs in the back of police cars on their way to the county jail.

CHAPTER FORTY-FIVE

BACK AT THE HOSPITAL, BRENT was just finishing his full confession to Jed and Jackson. He told them everything, from the moment Mike had picked him up on his way home from church. He told them the lies that Frank Snelling had told about T.J. and the knife. He told them how Sean had only said he was going to deliver a message. He told them how he screamed when he saw the gun and lunged at Mike's arm when he shot. And he told them why he hadn't gone to the police—he was scared of Sean and the threat he had made.

"Geez, I thought *I* was having a bad week," said Jackson under his breath.

Jed couldn't believe it. All this time, Brent had known who shot T.J.! Brent had been in the car when it happened! He'd known exactly what was going on in the barn. No wonder he hadn't wanted to flag down the Deputy; he was afraid of what would happen to his mom. No wonder Brent had been acting so strange. He believed everything was his fault. Jed wasn't happy that Brent had been so untruthful for so long, but he wasn't angry either. He knelt down in front of his friend and tightened his hands against Brent's limp arms.

"Brent," Jed said, "T.J. will forgive you." He waited for Brent to look up at his eyes. "When you say you're sorry like you just did, he accepts. It's done. That's the way it is with a true Christian, you know. That's why you don't have to punish yourself for the rest of your life."

"Remember that time when you got locked out of your house and T.J. climbed through the cat door for you?" asked Jackson. Brent chuckled a little bit.

"Remember when you hid in his locker and he spit grape juice all over your face?" Jed added.

"And my new white shoes." Brent remembered.

"You've got history with T.J. He knows you," Jed said. "He will understand; he always has."

Jed's mind bounced back to his computer screen. "By the way, I got another message from him tonight," he said.

"What did it say?" asked Jackson.

"Said, 'It's getting better. Pray again.'"

Brent took a deep breath. "You think this means he's alive?"

"If T.J. says to pray, then we're gonna keep praying." Jackson said. He paused, "Jed, you pray."

"Let's do it," Brent said.

"Okay." Jed moved to the head of T.J.'s bedside. He knelt down and took his friend's head in his hands. He paused and breathed a deep breath. "Jesus, we ask You to come," Jed prayed. "We ask for Your Holy Spirit, Lord."

Jackson and Brent stood at the end of the bed by T.J.'s feet. Brent put his arm around Jackson as Jed began to pray. Jackson, the Mouth, began to broadcast the prayer play-by-play.

"And as Jed starts prayin', God starts workin'," Jackson said.

"Shhh," Brent said, and he whapped Jackson on the side of the head.

But Jackson didn't stop. "And T.J.'s brain is startin' to wake up."

"Jackson, shut up," Brent said. "He's trying to pray."

Jed wasn't distracted at all. He just kept praying. "Father, we ask for Your will here Lord…"

"And Brent tells him to shut up," Jackson said, "But he doesn't cause we're on a roll here."

"Jackson," Brent said, "Seriously, shut up, or I'm going to beat the crap out of you."

"We just want you to be glorified, God." Jed was still praying.

"And there have been many martyrs in Christian history, and Jackson may soon be on that list," Jackson said.

Brent was laughing now, "Jackson, seriously, shut up."

"God, we want You to heal T.J.," Jed prayed.

"But he's not going to shut up," Jackson said, "because the brain machine starts to beep, and beep, and beep."

Right then, in the midst of Jed's prayer, or maybe it was Jackson's prayer or Brent's prayer, a machine *did* start to beep. Through the normal whirring and hisses of the machines came a new and intrusive beeping sound. All three boys turned to see what it was.

"Look!" yelled Brent.

The EEG had come to life. The screen that had been totally blank for weeks was suddenly full of horizontal lines, and the lines were dancing.

"Look!" Brent said.

Nurse Sandy was back in the room in no time.

"Boys, boys, I need everyone out of the room now."

Dr. Boss was close behind her.

CHAPTER FORTY-SIX

Jackson, Jed, and Brent backed away from the bed as people in uniforms came rushing into the room. The space was soon swarming with startled faces—nurses, doctors, and specialists ready to investigate. The boys were pushed out and asked to leave the intensive care unit.

Confused and excited—but trying not to become too excited— Jed continued to pray silently as he walked. *What are You doing God?* he asked. Nervousness welled up in his body. *Is this for real?*

The boys walked down the empty corridor outside the ICU and headed in the general direction of the waiting room. They were eager to share the news of the beeping with someone, with anyone. They walked with a brisk and enthusiastic pace, and just as they reached the end of the corridor they stopped dead in their tracks.

From out of nowhere, seemingly, stepped Sean O'Sullivan and his burly bodyguard. Sean, complete with his signature black leather coat and bowler hat, was standing right in front of Brent. Instantly, the jovial moment was punctured with fear.

"Brent, I've been looking for you," Sean said with a smirk in his voice. "We need to have a little talk you and I. Someplace more private."

"I think this is private enough," Brent answered.

Sean chuckled a little bit. "We had an arrangement, Brent. And I'm still happy to keep my end of the bargain as long as you keep yours."

Jackson stepped up and extended his hand to Sean. "Hi, I'm Jackson, what's your name?"

"This is none of your business," Sean responded. He ignored the hand.

"His name's Sean," Jed said.

"You know this guy?" Jackson asked.

"I've heard of him," Jed said.

"Well, he seems to have some attitude issues," Jackson said, raising his eyebrows.

Brent kept his eyes locked on Sean and formed a plan in his mind. He needed to get in close.

"No, don't worry about him, Jackson," Brent said. "He's just not potty trained."

Sean stepped closer to Brent, "You think I'm joking?"

Brent answered firmly, "No. I think you *are* a joke."

Sean was livid. He wasn't used to being insulted – especially by a fifteen-year-old kid. Sean grabbed Brent by the shoulders and slammed him against the corridor wall.

Sean was small but incredibly strong. Brent was pinned against the wall, and he couldn't move his arms. Sean glared at him.

"We'll meet again 'eh, someplace more private. You won't be able to find me, but don't worry—I'll find you."

Brent had him right where he wanted him. With Sean distracted and aggressive, Brent was able to discretely pull the remaining tracker out of his pants pocket and slip it into the front left pocket of Sean's leather coat. Once that was done, Brent shoved back and cleared himself from Sean's grip.

Sean let him go, but he leaned in close to Brent's face for one final threat.

"Give your momma a kiss for me," he said.

"Yeah, yeah I'll do that," Brent said.

Sean held his menacing stare and looked Brent right in the eye, but Brent never flinched. His courage seemed to cause a flicker of doubt in Sean's silicon exterior. Brent wasn't reacting to his threats like Sean expected him to, so he leaned in even closer and made an exaggerated smooching sound with his lips. Then he and his menacing bodyguard turned and walked away.

Brent watched him go, and when they were finally out the emergency exit doors he exhaled and fell back against the wall.

"That's an angry leprechaun," Jackson said. They all laughed.

Brent pulled out his cell phone and dialed the Sheriff.

"Sheriff, listen, Sean came to the hospital."

"When?" Sheriff McDonald immediately asked.

"Just now, but I put the tracker in his pocket."

"Davis," the Sheriff called for his deputy, then he turned back to talk on his phone to Brent. "He's got it on him right now?"

"Yeah. I didn't have much time," Brent answered.

"Atta boy, Brent! Follow the bait, Deputy. We got a tracker! He's going to lead us right to the big fish. Dial that frequency and bring him in." Sheriff McDonald had a big smile on his face.

Jed threw his hands on Brent's shoulders.

"Dude, you put a tracker in his pocket?" Jed said, laughing.

"Yeah," Brent said, as he folded over in half, releasing all his nervous energy.

"Babe," Jed said. He and Jackson both gave Brent a hug.

"Well, the good news is," Jackson said to Brent, "If he would have hit you in the face, at least you'd be right across the hall from the emergency room."

"Or like this," Jackson said. He threw Jed up against the wall just like Sean had done to Brent and said in a threatening tone and bad Irish accent, "Your tie is crooked." Then he pursed his lips and made a smooching sound. They laughed hard.

:]

Outside the hospital, Sean and his driver got into the Audi Q7 and took off, expecting to leave Charlevoix and never look back. They didn't get far. On US 31, just four miles south of town, the Audi suddenly found itself surrounded by a trio of sheriff cars.

Sean sat dumbfounded. *There was no way...* Then he reached into his coat pocket. He pulled out two one hundred dollar bills wrapped around a small, peanut-sized metallic device.

CHAPTER FORTY-SEVEN

AT 10:45 P.M. A TWIN engine Cessna landed at the Charlevoix Municipal Airport. Two men got off the plane, one carrying a small black satchel, the other a white medical cooler with a Red Cross sticker on it. Butch Kooyer was waiting to greet them. He ran out onto the tarmac and welcomed them to Charlevoix the Beautiful. But he had bad news for them.

"There will be no harvesting of organs here tonight," Butch said. "T.J. will be needing them himself. I'm truly sorry, but I'm also really happy for our friend. T.J." He wished them a nice flight home.

After a few moments and a quick phone call, the two men walked straight back to the plane. The pilot hadn't even turned his lights off.

:)

By midnight a crowd had gathered at the hospital waiting room. Jed's mom had been working the phones, calling everyone on the prayer chain. She apologized for calling so late, but she

225

wanted them to know that there had been an unexpected flutter of brain activity and that the organ harvest had been cancelled.

The word had spread quickly. Reverend Lewis, Jordyn, the Brackens, Sandy Carlson, Lois Fencett, Coach Howell (wearing his Rayders warm up), Butch Kooyer, Bucky, Marcos, Hayden, Lyndon and most of the guys from the basketball team, three girls from the cheerleading squad, Mr. Klein the principal, Sheriff McDonald, and, of course, the Frontier Boys, all waited anxiously in the crowded waiting room.

Finally a door opened, and Dr. Craig Boss emerged to address the group.

"Excuse me, can I have your attention, please? I do have a bit of news for you."

The room instantly hushed.

"I just spoke with T.J., and he's complaining of a small headache, but he's going to make it through."

Instantly a cheer of unbridled joy erupted through the lobby. A headache! They had never heard more joyous news. Everyone started hugging each another, giving high fives, and letting loose emotions that had been bottled up for weeks. Reverend Lewis fell to the ground in relief and gratitude. Tears fell and shouts of thanksgiving echoed through the pandemonium.

In the joyous fray, Jordyn found Jed. He gave her a huge hug. "It's amazing!" Jed said.

"Amazing," Jordyn said, with tears in her eyes. She gave him another hug.

"Hey Jed, when you see T.J., don't tell him I was reading his journals, okay?

"His journals?" Jed asked, not understanding.

"Yeah, what I sent you online."

"Those messages were from you?" Jed's eyes widened.

"I told you that. I told you in the first message."

"I did not get that. I thought they were from T.J.," Jed said.

"Well, they were. They were from his journals, from his time in Ghana. I thought that T.J. would want you to know who he really was. And, since you didn't respond I just—wait, you thought they were from *T.J.,* T.J.?"

Jed nodded.

"Jed, that would be weird."

"Tell me about it."

"So don't tell him, all right?"

"He's going to find out."

"Not if you don't tell him."

"I told Jackson," said Jed. Jordyn rolled her eyes.

Jackson heard his name. He came over.

"Told me what?"

Jed just laughed and gave him a huge bear hug.

CHAPTER FORTY-EIGHT

ON THE FOLLOWING TUESDAY MORNING 264 people crammed into a small white Lutheran church in Eden Prairie, Minnesota. The sun was bright, and its rays shone directly through the left side windows to warm the black shirts and jackets of the people whose backs were to the walls. They were at the funeral of Valerie Lee, who had died in her hospital bed just two days earlier. She needed a new heart, a new heart that never came.

The pews were filled with classmates, uncles, aunts, cousins, grandparents, teachers, and friends. Valerie's volleyball coach and piano teacher sat together near the back of the room, and kids from her youth group played a slideshow of pictures of her life, from the day she was born until the week before she left. She had been dearly loved, and she was fiercely missed.

Valerie's mother and father stood together in the first row. Tears streamed from their faces for the full seventy-five minutes of the service. They had lost their only daughter. A void had been created that would never be filled.

A classmate played the piano while the congregation sang Valerie's favorite hymn––"In Christ Alone." Mr. and Mrs. Lee,

tears unceasing, grabbed one another's hands as they sang the final verse:

No guilt in life, no fear in death—

This is the pow'r of Christ in me;

From life's first cry to final breath,

Jesus commands my destiny.

No pow'r of hell, no scheme of man,

Can ever pluck me from His hand;

Till He returns or calls me home—

Here in the pow'r of Christ I'll stand.

Though the bitterness of their loss pierced their stomachs like a lance, they sang the song with hope and conviction. Their hope was based in the resurrection of Christ and the promise of the gospel. It was the hope of Heaven.

CHAPTER FORTY-NINE

THE SNOWS OF JANUARY WERE followed by an even colder February. But March, as she is known to do, came in like a lion and went out like a lamb. By early April only a few icy remnants of the long winter remained, and every day the ice chunks bobbing in the cold waters by the shoreline were shrinking. Lake Michigan was succumbing to warmer waters.

Jed, Brent, and Jackson were playing basketball down by the lakeshore. T.J. was there too, in his wheelchair. The guys included him in their pick-up game of two-on-two. T.J. in a wheelchair was probably still a better basketball player than Jackson on two feet. Jackson, however, continued to provide the play-by-play.

"This team's got heart, baby," said Jackson in his best Dick Vitale, "I just don't see anyone stopping them. They've got it all. They've got scoring. They've got defense. They've got the guy sitting in the wheelchair who can still shoot the three ball... It's unbelievable, baby. What can I tell you?"

Jed picked up a rebound and tossed the ball up to Jackson, who passed it to T.J. He wasn't supposed to stand for another six weeks, but he couldn't wait. With a little help from his buddies,

T.J. slowly rose out of the chair. He had a huge grin on his face as he shot the ball.

Swish.

Standing together next to the melting ice of Lake Michigan the four boys embraced. They were together, united, and young. The frontier before them was as wide and limitless as a great lake horizon, as unpredictable as tomorrow.

:]

Jed wrote in his own journal that night:

> *T.J.'s going to be okay. He's not supposed to be up and walking for another six weeks, but he says he's a fast healer, and seeing how fast he runs, I kind of trust him.*
>
> *Brent's brother Mike is going to spend a couple of years in prison, and the cops caught Sean a few miles out of town as he was running away.*
>
> *We're not exactly sure what loving our enemies looks like here, but T.J.'s not holding any grudges, and he's actually visited Mike already.*
>
> *Jackson—he's got me laughing every thirty seconds again, and Brent, well—I love that guy.*
>
> *As for me, I think I'm learning to appreciate each day a little bit more.*
>
> *I read something cool. In Joshua, it says, "Do not be afraid, do not be discouraged, for the Lord your God will be with you wherever you go." Yeah—He's good.*

232

SPECIAL THANKS

To Jeff Barker for his invaluable assistance on the screenplay for The Frontier Boys, all of which worked its way back into this manuscript, and to Karen Barker for the low rent writing room in the former garage.

To all the actors who gave their voices to these characters in the film The Frontier Boys. In many cases your ad libs are now recorded on these pages as dialogue. Thank you Sam Kenny, Greg Myhre, Jake Boyce, Rodney Wiseman, Ted Swartz, Tim Lofing, and the whole great lot of you.

To the team at Grooters Productions and AngelHouse Media who bring excellence every day to everything you do, to everything we do together. You are all more than colleagues – you are co-workers for the kingdom.

To Anisa Williams, who keeps me and the whole team moving in the right direction.

To Jed Grooters, my son, with whom this story was first conceived on that ski trip many years ago, and with whom the film was made. This is your story as much as it is mine. To my beloved daughter, Jordyn Osburn, whose reviews and edits made every page better.

To Joel Nori and the whole team at Destiny Image® Publishers who have come behind The Frontier Boys and helped introduce them to people all around the world.

To my beautiful and talented wife Judy who has supported this endeavor in every practical way possible. Thank you for being the inspiration for whoever wrote Proverbs 31. Don't know how they foresaw you so clearly...

And mostly thanks, in case you're reading this, to Jesus of Nazareth. Your life and sacrifice is the driving force behind everything we do, we see, we taste, and we hear – whether we dumb humans know it or not. May we be one as you and the Father are one.

ABOUT JOHN GROOTERS

John Grooters is the author of *The Frontier Boys*, the writer and director of the film by the same name, and the author of the non-fiction book *Raising a Modern Frontier Boy*. His work as a writer, director, and producer on film, broadcast and non-broadcast media projects has earned numerous national and international awards for creative and production excellence. He is the guitar half of the Christian Rock duo Grooters & Beal. Father of two, John is an avid sports fan, a modestly successful Little League coach, a passionate student of the Bible, and a dusty follower of Jesus.

IN THE RIGHT HANDS, THIS BOOK WILL CHANGE LIVES!

Most of the people who need this message will not be looking for this book. To change their lives, you need to put a copy of this book in their hands.

> *But others (seeds) fell into good ground, and brought forth fruit, some a hundred-fold, some sixty-fold, some thirty-fold* (Matthew 13:8).

Our ministry is constantly seeking methods to find the good ground, the people who need this anointed message to change their lives. Will you help us reach these people?

> *Remember this—a farmer who plants only a few seeds will get a small crop. But the one who plants generously will get a generous crop* (2 Corinthians 9:6).

EXTEND THIS MINISTRY BY SOWING
3 BOOKS, 5 BOOKS, 10 BOOKS, OR MORE TODAY,
AND BECOME A LIFE CHANGER!

Thank you,

Don Nori Sr., Founder
Destiny Image
Since 1982

DESTINY IMAGE PUBLISHERS, INC.

"Promoting Inspired Lives."

VISIT OUR NEW SITE HOME AT
WWW.DESTINYIMAGE.COM

FREE SUBSCRIPTION TO DI NEWSLETTER

Receive free unpublished articles by top DI authors, exclusive
discounts, and free downloads from our best and newest books.
Visit www.destinyimage.com to subscribe.

Write to: Destiny Image
P.O. Box 310
Shippensburg, PA 17257-0310

Call: 1-800-722-6774

Email: orders@destinyimage.com

For a complete list of our titles or to place an order
online, visit www.destinyimage.com.

FIND US ON FACEBOOK OR FOLLOW US ON TWITTER.

www.facebook.com/destinyimage   facebook
www.twitter.com/destinyimage   twitter